"Lacy and I are pretty used to the way things are now,"

Joel told Megan. "I don't want you to—I'd rather you didn't—"

"Interfere?" Indignation warmed Megan's face, had her leveling her gaze on him.

"If that's how you want to say it." Joel's eyes lit with a gleam that dropped ten years from his appearance. His slow perusal made her blood heat in her veins. "You've grown up, Megan."

The irreverent thought crossed her mind that she wished she could show him just how much. But then, she thought wryly, her innocence would hardly impress him. He'd want a woman who'd learned how to please a man.

But the way he was looking at her had all kinds of possibilities coming to mind. She would know what to do. Know what she wanted him to do....

Dear Reader,

As Celebration 1000! moves into its third exciting month, Silhouette Romance is pleased to present a very special book from one of your all-time favorite authors, Debbie Macomber! In *The Bachelor Prince,* a handsome prince comes to America in search of a bride to save his country from ruin. But falling for the wrong woman made his duty a struggle. Was loving Hope Jordan worth losing his kingdom?

If you enjoyed Laurie Paige's WILD RIVER books in the Special Edition line, don't miss *A Rogue's Heart,* as Silhouette Romance carries on this series of rough-and-ready men and the women they love.

No celebration would be complete without a FABULOUS FATHER. This month, Gayle Kaye tells the heartwarming story of a five-year-old ballerina-in-the-making who brings her pretty dance teacher and her overprotective dad together for some very private lessons.

Get set for love—and laughter—in two wonderful new books: *Housemates* by Terry Essig and *The Reluctant Hero* by Sandra Paul. And be sure to look for debut author Robin Nicholas's emotional story of a woman who must choose between the man she loves and the town she longs to leave in *The Cowboy and His Lady.*

Next month, the celebration continues with books by beloved authors Annette Broadrick and Elizabeth August. Thanks so much for joining us during this very special event.

Happy reading!

Anne Canadeo
Senior Editor

Please address questions and book requests to:
Reader Service
U.S.: P.O. Box 1325, Buffalo, NY 14269
Canadian: P.O. Box 1050, Niagara Falls, Ont. L2E 7G7

THE COWBOY
AND HIS LADY
Robin Nicholas

Silhouette
ROMANCE™

Published by Silhouette Books

America's Publisher of Contemporary Romance

To Terry, Linda, Kim and Sue,
and to all of Chapter 78, my teachers and friends.

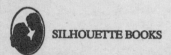 SILHOUETTE BOOKS

ISBN 0-373-19017-4

THE COWBOY AND HIS LADY

Copyright © 1994 by Robin Kapala

This edition published by arrangement with Harlequin Enterprises B.V.

® and TM are trademarks of Harlequin Enterprises B.V., used under license. Trademarks indicated with ® are registered in the United States Patent and Trademark Office, the Canadian Trade Marks Office and in other countries.

Printed in U.S.A.

ROBIN NICHOLAS

lives in Illinois. She and her husband, Dan, keep busy raising their son, Nick, and racing harness horses.

A Note from the Author

A belief in happy endings led me to Silhouette Romance as a writer just as it has drawn readers back time and again.

If I have a special goal in writing, it is to write a book that touches your heart, one you'll want to read again. With that goal in mind, I have written the story of Joel, Megan and Lacy.

I am pleased to celebrate the sale of my first book in connection with the Silhouette Romance line's celebration of book 1000.

Thank you for your support of my first effort.

Sincerely,

Robin Nicholas

Chapter One

His cowboy's silhouette stretched across dry summer grass as Joel Crawford distanced himself from South Dakota's Belle Fourche Rodeo Arena. A sweat-glistened bay trailed behind him as he led his horse through a maze of trucks and trailers to his own black and silver rig. He'd roped in the slack, trading the slot he'd drawn in the night's rodeo to take his turn in the heat of the day before an empty grandstand. But the notion that he'd need a night away from the bright lights and the crowd didn't wash anymore. What he needed was to go home.

Drawing up alongside his silver four-horse trailer, Joel dropped the reins, watching as Tally propped a foreleg, the horse's nostrils ruffling in a soft nicker. Taking a similar two-legged stance, Joel sighed, thumbs hitched in the pockets of well-worn jeans. He and Tally both needed a rest.

Joel leaned tiredly against the pickup, plucking a straw from the bale in back and wishing he had one of the cigarettes he'd given up.

He was twenty-eight years old with a battered body that felt closer to fifty and a heart that might never have felt young again if it wasn't for his four-year-old daughter, Lacy. He couldn't imagine a life without her, hard as it sometimes was with her.

"Joel!"

His head came up, the bell-like ring of Lacy's voice carrying from the grandstand as she ran toward him. His daughter had been blessed with coltish legs hell-bent on taking her through life at a full gallop. Joel watched her, his pride edged with pain. The mane of yellow hair streaming behind her never failed to remind him of his ex-wife, Luann.

There were only hints of his own tawny hair streaked through Lacy's, but they shared the same slate-blue eyes, and her straight nose was a delicate version of his own. To his regret, she refused to call him Daddy. If the rest of the world called him Joel, she would, too. Considering her four-year-old logic, Joel figured he was lucky she hadn't called him worse. Bending down, he caught her on the run, scooping her up with one arm. When she wrapped her small arms around his neck, the title didn't seem to matter.

"You hungry, Lacy?"

Lacy plucked the straw from her father's mouth and placed it between her tiny pearl-white teeth. "I want a hot dog."

Lacy always wanted a hot dog. He figured he was lucky she had a similar penchant for apples and milk. Joel set her down and opened the truck door, fishing his wallet from beneath the seat. He pulled out some money and turned to find Lacy tickling Tally's nose with the straw, the horse patiently lipping at air as the little girl kept it just out of reach.

"Don't tease Tally, Lacy."

Relenting, she fed the straw to the horse. "Did you and Tally win today?"

"Not today." Joel crouched to her level, waiting as she gave the horse a comforting pat, thinking he could use a little consoling, too. As if reading his mind, Lacy cuddled close. Joel buried his face in her hair, suddenly feeling the fear that only a parent could know, asking a prayer that only a parent could need. He made himself release her.

"How about going to the food stand, right over there, and getting us some lunch? Think you can handle that?"

"I can do it."

Joel tucked the money in Lacy's pocket and she darted off, her golden hair and pink shirt bobbing as she skipped through the grass. Joel's heart lurched when she fell and he watched uneasily as she clambered up, rump first like a calf. After a moment, she turned to wave at him, twin dark stains of God knew what on the knees of her jeans. Joel waved back and let out a long, slow breath as she skipped across the field.

He gazed after her, a little envious, a bit disturbed. Lacy seemed so untouched by it all—her mother's desertion, the divorce. Regret darkened his eyes. He was slowly coming to the conclusion that Lacy couldn't miss what she'd never really had.

Joel rocked his hat to the back of his head. Two years had passed since Luann left. She was still on the circuit, pursuing her love of barrel racing and building a reputation for sleeping around. His sense of failure often weighed more heavily than he could bear. But when he looked at his motherless daughter and remembered Luann's heartless departure, her bold scrawl as she'd signed over custody, a bitterness took hold that buried all but the need to protect his child.

Keeping a watchful eye on Lacy, Joel stowed his gear and brushed Tally down. He wrapped the horse's legs, thinking some time out to pasture wouldn't hurt the old horse. Unfolding stiff knees, he decided it wouldn't hurt him, either.

Done with his chores, Joel headed toward Lacy, her arms cradling a red-and-white carton. Joel slowed, then stopped. He watched her careful steps, his heart and his throat in a sudden knot. His baby girl was growing up.

Two great events loomed in the near future for Lacy and for him. Her birthday, and at the end of next month, school. She wanted a doll that cost more than the fifty dollars he had in his pocket and she wanted new pink jeans for the first day of school. He guessed he could handle that. It was all the questions she had about where she would go to school—how she would go to school—that had him worried. Even at her tender age, Lacy realized life revolved around the next rodeo.

Since his father's death six years ago, he'd had no reason to go home to Paradise. Now the time had come to provide a home base for Lacy, even if it meant cutting back on rodeos. The Miller Tack Shop in Paradise was for sale. He had a small savings tucked away in the Paradise Bank. Coupled with a loan, he could buy the business. The store could provide a way to supplement his earnings and allow him to make an investment in Lacy's future.

They met toe to toe in the field and Joel reached down and lifted Lacy, carton and all, her scuffed white boots brushing his hips as her legs dangled. They ambled toward the rig, sipping cola from straws, his hat brim shading her sunburned nose from the relentless rays at their backs. Reaching for memories, he shared them with Lacy, and hoped she'd want to go home to the Nebraska farm where he'd grown up.

Megan Miller pushed open the tack shop door, her keys and a milk shake cradled in one hand, a newspaper and an assortment of mail clutched in the other. Edging inside, she elbowed the door shut, using the corner of the paper to flip the Open sign to the appropriate side for the afternoon hours. She didn't bother with the lights for the long low room was flooded with sunlight, dust motes dancing in the hot beams that crept beneath the outside awning and streamed through the windows.

Crossing to her desk behind the counter, Megan made quick work of freeing her hands and turned on the phone's answering machine, hoping her father had left word that the store was sold. But there was no call from Arizona, where her father and sister had recently moved; her father to seek relief from his allergies, Suzanne to attend college this fall.

Megan sank to the leather chair before the desk. Two weeks ago, her dad had phoned to tell her someone had finally shown a real interest in the tack shop. He'd sworn she would be free to go in another month if the sale went through. Now, each day that passed seemed endless. She'd already waited years to be free of this store, this town and the small farm down the road. Fifteen years to be exact.

Megan could still remember the day her mother, Patrice, had left them, when Suzanne had been four and she had been ten. Suzanne had grasped her sister's hand and held on tight and Megan had somehow stepped into adulthood, taking the place of a mother they'd never heard from again. She remembered her dad gazing at them as if they'd been beamed down from another planet. She imagined they'd looked at him much the same way. He'd always been out in the fields or working away at the endless chores on the farm. Somehow, in the years that followed, the three of them had become a family. But she'd never lost the resolve to someday find her mother.

Megan sifted through the mix of mail. There was a large brown envelope from Suzanne, and Megan opened it to find a fashion magazine. An affectionate laugh escaped. Suzanne knew Megan wanted a new look before she left Paradise. Her sister also knew she hadn't the faintest idea of how to achieve that.

Sighing, Megan thumbed through the magazine. Glancing at the pictures of the sophisticated models, she fingered her dark braid, a short version of the one she'd worn as a kid. Her sister had been the one who dated and knew how to dress and act.

Even at the age of four, Suzanne had been a little princess, pleasing their mother while Megan disappointed her with her tomboy ways. Suzanne was everything Patrice had been. Polished and poised. Everything Megan was not.

Megan folded the magazine closed. That would all change, once she left Paradise. One thing she could do was take pictures. She planned to freelance, to have her name captioned beneath the photos of a pictorial essay in a famous magazine. Millions would see. Maybe even Patrice...

Tap. Tap. Tap.

Startled, Megan looked toward the wooden counter perpendicular to her desk. She had been—and still appeared to be—alone in the shop. When the tapping came again, Megan lowered her gaze, peering through the glass cabinet below the countertop. From the other side of an array of jewelry, spurs and genuine leather wallets, a small girl looked back at her.

Pert nose pressed to the glass, the girl regarded Megan without so much as a blink. Feeling a bit like a window display, Megan stared back. Except for the sunburn on the child's nose, Megan might have been looking at a doll. One with long-lashed blue-gray eyes and a wealth of yellow hair. Rosebud lips curved in a smile, revealing tiny, white teeth. Megan's mouth curved in response.

Rising, Megan walked over to the counter. Many of the neighborhood kids dropped in to use the gumball machine. Some days, she swore it took in more than the store.

Megan rested her arms on the countertop. Her smile grew wary. The child's white western boots were similar to the scarred cream-colored boots she herself wore. They each had on frosted jeans, and though her cropped T-shirt was a darker pink than the girl's, it was a T-shirt all the same. Megan could only sigh over the fact that she was twenty-five years old and dressed like a four-year-old.

"May I help you, young lady?"

"I need some change, please. I want to buy gum."

"Coming right up."

Megan felt the blue eyes watching her as she popped open the cash box drawer. She drew out some coins and placed them in the little girl's hand, taking a quarter in exchange.

The child stared at the dimes and nickel in her hand. After a moment, Megan chuckled, realizing she was counting her change. Finally satisfied, she chirped, "Thank you," and went over to the gumball machine by the door.

"You're welcome," Megan answered, wondering who the girl belonged to. She knew most of the kids by sight and a few by name, but she was sure she'd never seen this little angel before.

Thinking the girl seemed rather young to be alone, Megan came from behind the counter, slipping between racks of saddles on display to look out one of the shop's wide front windows. Outside, the brown and white Miller Tack Shop sign swung gently on its hinges over the door, reflecting the hot July sun back at the sky. Her blue pickup sat in the row of parking spaces that ran the length of the redwood bungalow. Parked beside it was a black and silver Chevy truck bearing South Dakota plates, with a silver four-horse in tow. Reaching into the back of the Chevy was a cowgirl's dream.

Thick straight hair the color of wheat sprang from beneath a straw hat to frame a face of chiseled perfection. A turquoise feather, set in the hat's band, fanned in unison to the sudden flutter of Megan's heart. The cowboy pulled a saddle from the truck bed, dangling it by the pommel as if it weighed no more than a saddle blanket, tanned biceps flexing against a gray T-shirt that hung loosely over his jeans. He swung around, blue eyes catching her gaze through the window.

Recognition dawned like a slow, unfolding sunrise within her. In her mind, his face was that of a high school senior, the look in his eye a little more wild, the stance a little more restless. Her heart thudded, much as it used to when she'd watched Joel Crawford from a distance.

He stared, and she had a sense of seeing herself through his eyes, making her aware of that tiny cowlick in her bangs, the ink stain above her breast pocket. Her toes curled in her boots, and she felt the breeze from the fan overhead cooling the damp back of her neck as she waited to see if he would recognize her. When he smiled at her, a shiver skimmed down her spine.

Joel headed for the store. Megan retreated behind the counter, certain she must have looked like the child had, peering through the glass cabinet. The tack shop door creaked open and Joel walked in, leaning down to exchange a word with the little girl.

She remembered then, the gossip about Joel's broken marriage. How the rodeo queen had left him for a string of other cowboys to raise his daughter alone. Looking at the little girl, Megan had no doubt this was Joel's child. The resemblance was too strong.

Curling her fingers into her palms, Megan watched him walk toward her, taking her in from the toes of her boots to her bangs. It was a brief, inoffensive glance, yet Megan felt a girlish fluster.

Discreetly, she made her own survey and decided he'd changed. He now had a slow easy walk, though his step was more tired than lazy, his lean torso slightly curved to accommodate the weight of the saddle. She'd always thought him almost pretty, his too-long hair rich and shiny, his mouth wide and full. As he neared the counter, a sheen of sweat became visible above his upper lip and Megan tried not to stare. Like the child, his blue eyes bordered on gray, but where the girl's had been bright and lively, his held a weariness that said he'd been there, he'd seen it all. The impatience that had once burned in his eyes was gone.

Joel stopped before the counter, resting the saddle against his knee. Then he grinned. "You haven't changed a bit, Megan Miller."

At least he had some memory of her. He'd been three years her senior and she had admired him from afar with no expectations of his ever noticing her. She could even remember one time when she'd hoped he wouldn't notice her. The hot summer day seemed burned in her memory. Riding her bike by the Crawford farm on her way to run an errand in town, she'd seen Joel standing shirtless on a hayrack in the field. The sight of his gold gleaming skin had arrested her gaze and landed her in a ditch. She'd climbed from beneath her bike and pedaled furiously toward town with bloody knees, hoping he hadn't seen her.

Megan's cheeks heated with the thought. Trying to ease past the awkwardness she felt, she nodded toward Lacy. "She looks just like you."

Joel half turned to look at his daughter, murmuring, "Except for the hair."

Luann. His wife's name had been Luann. There'd been a grainy photo of them once in the *Paradise Review*. Joel and a glamorous blonde.

"Lacy, say hello to Miss Miller."

Megan smiled at Lacy, who called a hello from beside the gumball machine. Feeling more comfortable, she asked, "What brings you back to Paradise?"

He slowly faced her, shifting the weight of the saddle to rest more easily against his knee. His expression seemed to hold a hint of puzzlement. "I'm moving back onto the farm," he said.

"My father and Suzanne recently moved to Arizona, so I'm left to keep things under control." Megan edged from behind the counter, looking pointedly at the saddle he carried. It had the high horn of a roping saddle and looked well used. "I can handle any repairs you might need."

"That would be fine. New stirrup straps and a cinch should take care of it." Joel leaned down to prop the saddle near her feet. When he straightened, he stood closer, the musky scent of him filling her nostrils. He hitched his thumbs in the snug front pockets of his jeans. "Actually, I knew your dad had moved. I'd heard he was selling the store."

"He finally has an interested buyer." Funny, how Joel had come home to Paradise just when she was finally able to leave. Megan made herself smile. "I was beginning to think I was going to be stuck here forever."

"I remember that feeling." His tone made it seem a long time ago. His hat brim tilted fractionally. "I never took you for the type to want to leave."

Megan stiffened, affronted. He remembered her, but obviously as some small-town girl who could never be anything else. "It so happens, I'll be leaving as soon as the store is sold. I've done some freelance photography and I plan to make a career of it."

There was a pause, then Joel asked, "Where will you go?"

"California." She could still remember the plane ticket clutched in her mother's hand, the only lead she had to Patrice's whereabouts. Aware she'd sounded abrupt, Megan softened her answer with a smile.

"So you're pretty happy about selling the store," Joel stated. Before she could do more than nod, he went on, "I suppose it will be okay if I give you the news, then. I'm the one who's buying the tack shop."

Megan stood stock-still, but her mind raced. She'd barely absorbed the fact that Joel was back in town. Now he was telling her he was buying the store. Why hadn't her father phoned to give her the good news? "How?" she finally breathed. "When?"

"I was in touch with the bank here in Paradise a couple weeks ago. It came around in conversation that your dad wanted to sell. I gave Matt a call." Joel shrugged. "I was looking to buy, he was looking to sell. He's supposed to be here in town sometime next week so I can look over the books and get familiar with the store. Since I don't foresee any problems, we'll probably sign the papers while he's here."

Unbelievable. When Joel had left ten years ago, she hadn't expected he would be back. No one had. There were some, especially those with teenage daughters, who'd breathed a sigh of relief. He hadn't been a troublemaker, exactly, but he'd been an odd mix of restlessness and maturity that his peers held in awe and their parents observed with apprehension. It was hard to fathom that he'd leave the rodeo circuit to come home, buy a business and settle down.

The only time she'd known Joel to return had been for his father's funeral, six years ago. She'd caught a glimpse of him as he'd passed through town, handsome in a dove-gray suit. Through the store's windows, she had seen the pain etched on his face; the same pain she remembered seeing when he was fifteen and his mother had passed away. He'd left Paradise as soon as his father's funeral was over, and word that he'd married followed soon after. Two years ago, he'd divorced. Megan's gaze drifted to Lacy. The child, she suspected, was what had finally brought him home. It was hard to imagine Joel raising his daughter alone while following the rodeo circuit.

Joel swung his weight to one hip, his boot scraping the floor. Megan blushed, realizing that he waited for some kind of reply. "I'm sorry. I'm just trying to take all this good news in. If you'd like to look around the shop now, you're welcome to. I guess you know that Dad's only selling because of his health—his allergies. He hopes to open another store in Arizona. If there's anything I can do..."

Megan's voice trailed off as Joel gave her an indulgent smile. She was rattling on, but then, this *was* good news. She'd waited a long time, seeing Suzanne through high school, working in the store. Now she would be free to put her plans into action. She gave a quick laugh. "I can't believe I'll finally be able to leave Paradise."

Joel gave an uneasy frown. "Matt sort of promised me you'd be available to work for a while, until Lacy and I got settled in."

Megan felt her own frown forming, unhappy over the thought of a delay. But she'd always given her father a hand at the shop. If it would help get the business sold, she certainly wouldn't refuse now. "Of course, I can work a while. I wasn't going to be leaving for a couple of weeks, anyway."

Joel glanced toward Lacy, and Megan sensed something evasive in the move. Then he leveled his gaze on her, all hint of unease disappearing. "Your father agreed you'd run the shop for at least another couple of months."

Megan felt her pleasant expression fade. No wonder her father hadn't called. He and Joel must have had quite a conversation about her, deciding how convenient it would be if she kept running the store.

She knew her father didn't realize the depth of her plans—it would hurt him too much to know she needed to find her mother, despite all the love he'd given. But he knew how important her photography was to her. Knew how long she'd waited to leave. Flatly she told Joel, "Dad must have forgotten how soon I planned to leave."

Joel was unwavering. "Your father guaranteed your help. It was part of the deal. I need time to get settled in. I've got horses coming in next month and no fences around my pasture."

"Surely you can find someone else to run the cash register until—"

"I don't want someone to run the cash register. I *have* to have someone to run the store." *Or else.* The implication hung like a tangible threat between them, making it clear that the sale of the store hinged on her cooperation.

Megan raised her chin and her gaze locked with Joel's angry one. The gumball machine rattled in the ensuing silence.

"Dammit."

They both jumped, gazes drawn to the source of profanity. Stunned, Megan watched past the cowboy's shoulder as the little girl stood with her back to them, ponytail swaying as she jiggled the gumball machine.

"Dammit," she repeated.

To his credit, a dull red flush crept beneath Joel's tan. "Lacy!" he growled. "Don't swear like that."

"But, Joel, this dammit machine won't work!"

Joel?

"Lacy Jo!" He took a step then stopped. Megan leaned away as he swung back, his grim face inches from hers. "Excuse me," he muttered. Striding over to his daughter, Joel crouched to her level, speaking in a hushed tone. Lacy gave a sob and stood sniffling, occasionally giving a hushed reply.

Drawn by their whispers, Megan inched closer. Joel rose to fiddle with the machine and Lacy crowded close, hugging his leg, both of them standing with their backs to her now. She was intrigued by the bond they seemed to share, despite the fact Lacy called him Joel and swore like a miniature cowhand.

Minutes passed as Megan waited. She pushed her hands into her pockets, trying to disassociate herself from the tender scene. But Joel's murmurs seemed to tease and beckon and there was just no ignoring Lacy's shuddery little hiccups.

Finally, Joel turned to face her, with Lacy swiveling along, still attached to his leg. "There's a nickel caught in the machine."

Joel looked sheepish, yet somehow protective as he rested a hand atop Lacy's head. Megan felt something give inside her, a weakening that started in her heart and settled in her knees. She had the disquieting feeling she would never lose the picture of the two of them standing there, linked together, framed by an aura of love.

Not trusting her voice, Megan gave a nod. At her approach, they stepped aside, moving as a unit. Pulling a hairpin from her pocket, Megan pried it apart, leaning over the machine and sliding the pin on either side of the nickel caught in the slot. Pinching the hairpin closed, she carefully lifted the nickel out and handed it to Lacy.

Lacy stared at the coin, then blinked at Megan, her eyes bright blue stars, her mouth a round O of surprise. One shimmery tear escaped, rolling over her cheek. Without thinking, Megan reached out to brush it away.

Lacy's cheek puffed in a smile and Joel watched with a feeling akin to pain, trying, but unable to recall Luann's ever touching their child in more than the most perfunctory way. Trying to recall, but failing to remember, the last time Luann had really touched him....

Now here was Megan, drying Lacy's tears, her pretty face flushed with pleasure over the sight of his daughter's smile. She dug in her jeans pocket for a dime and slipped it in the gumball machine, her dark eyes sparkling at Lacy.

Megan's hair was shorter now than when he'd last seen her, but shiny as ever, the rich chocolate-colored strands tucked into a short thick braid. She leaned to twist the knob on the machine, spilling gum into the small cup of Lacy's hands, and Joel's gaze trailed over her slender, leggy body. He noted for the first time that she was dressed in similar garb as his daughter. But there the similarity ended. There were shapely curves beneath Megan's T-shirt and the short top revealed a tantalizing glimpse of her creamy, trim waist, her hips gently flaring below.

Lacy turned to him then, her face lit with delight. "I got two pinks," she cried. "And white. I don't like white, but you do, Joel." She stood on tiptoe, offering the gum, and Joel bent close, nipping it from Lacy's small fingers. He straightened to find Megan gazing at him, at his mouth, with a look that stirred an ache within him.

An ache he was learning to live with. With a grimace, Joel prodded Lacy, "What do you say?"

"Thank you." Lacy's eyes adored Megan and Joel frowned, some protective instinct kicking in, even as he struggled with his own appreciation of Megan.

"What else?"

Lacy tucked her chin. "I'm sorry I said a bad word."

Megan smiled at her forgivingly. "There's a cherry lollipop on my desk, if you want to go get it."

Lacy grinned and scampered off, disappearing behind the counter.

Joel steeled himself against the smile Megan wore for his daughter. Lacy's welfare was riding, in part, on the purchase of this store. Impatient, Joel turned on Megan. "Look, your father and I had an agreement. The way I see it, your travel plans are the only thing standing in the way of the sale."

"My *career* plans can hardly wait until you're able to move into your house. That place has been empty for six years!"

"Sam Powell has been looking after the farm for me."

"Sam Powell is eighty-five years old."

"I don't expect any major problems." *Eighty-five?* "At least not any I can't handle."

"You obviously haven't seen the place yet," Megan said cryptically.

"The house is probably in better shape than it looks from the road," Joel insisted, hoping it was true. He was tired of cheap motels.

"In that case, your only problem is finding someone who can run the store *and* keep the books while you build a fence."

Joel waved a hand in impatience. "That takes time. I'm hardly going to invest in the store just to turn management of it over to some incompetent stranger. Your father could see the sense in that."

"I think you gave my father little choice to do otherwise," Megan accused, and in that moment she was nothing of the shy girl Joel remembered.

Not certain how to deal with her accusation or with her, Joel snapped Lacy's name, drawing his daughter from behind the counter. He glared at Megan. "I think I'll look over the shop another time. After I've met with your father."

"Fine," Megan said in a clipped tone. "But you can be certain I'll be talking with Dad before then."

Joel caught Lacy's hand, trying to keep a grip on his temper. Abruptly, he turned to the door, holding it open for Lacy to pass through. Lacy balked, calling a garbled farewell, and Joel felt his face heat beneath Megan's scrutiny. He nudged Lacy out, his determined gaze meeting Megan's before he let the door bang shut behind him.

Chapter Two

Joel planted his boot on the front-porch step, the sagging plank reflecting the sudden sinking of his spirit. From the corner of his eye, he could see a withered vine creeping up the gray remains of a white trellis, the window above it covered with weathered plywood. The late-afternoon sun seemed to strip the last of the color from the peeling yellow paint of his house, giving it a bare, neglected look that filled him with guilt.

Dammit. He'd hired Sam, trusting the man to keep the place in good repair. Joel swung his gaze briefly to the makeshift paddock he'd rigged for Tally. Sam had warned him about the fences, but he hadn't expected rotting posts and downed barbed wire. A loose gutter knocked in the breeze and he craned his neck by looking up. Yep, he reminded himself, Sam Powell was an old man. He sighed. Apparently too old.

The phrase *settling in* had taken on new meaning. But he was determined to make it the home it once had been. Matt Miller had promised him two months. He needed at least that before he would be able to run the tack shop himself. Joel frowned, irked to think Megan had been right about the condition of the farm.

Though he'd known of her more than known her, Megan didn't seem the same sweet quiet girl he remembered. Selfish and irresponsible came to mind; she wouldn't even work in the store a couple months longer to help her ill father, and in turn help him. And he hadn't missed her shocked disapproval over Lacy's swearing and calling him Joel. As if baby-sitting her sister after the Millers' divorce made her some kind of expert on child care.

"Joel!"

Lacy's cranky voice drew him around in time to see her climb out of the truck where she'd been sleeping. She stumbled through the long stems of cut grass drying on the lawn from a recent mowing, her bangs plastered to her forehead in dark blond clumps. Her cheeks were flushed, her small eyebrows drawing together while her lip pushed out in a tired pout. When she leaned against his leg, Joel lifted her, resting his cheek against her hair. She needed a bath. Sam had seen that the gas and electricity were turned on, and even the phone hooked up. But Joel had his doubts that they would be staying here tonight.

"This our house?"

Joel sighed. "This is it, Lacy. You stay put a minute until I check things out inside."

Skirting the sag in the step, Joel pulled the key from his pocket to let himself inside. The door swung open and he stepped into a ray of light, hearing the unmistakable scuffle of mice.

It looked like a haunted house. Pale dustcovers over the furniture took on ghostly shapes in the dim light that filtered through grimy windows. Giant cobwebs floated in a whisper of draft. A wren fluttered on the banister of the stairs, then bulleted to the second floor.

Small arms clutched his leg, making him start. Joel looked down at Lacy in exasperation. He'd told her to wait. But his frown faded at the dubious look on her face. He wondered if Lacy would like to camp outside tonight, like they often did when they found a campsite close to the rodeo grounds. It couldn't be any worse than the Paradise Inn, famous for its lumpy beds and cold showers.

After braving the staircase, Joel shooed the bird out an upstairs window, deciding to worry later about how it had gotten in. He returned downstairs to the single bathroom the old house boasted, mopping the floor and scrubbing the tub with an old shirt. Once it was as clean as he could manage, he filled it with water. Threading the pink band from Lacy's ponytail, Joel knelt on the hardwood floor to wash her hair, silently cursing knees that had run down the rope too many times in too many rodeos. He poured a dollop of shampoo on Lacy's head, thinking he'd put up the tent while she played in the tub a few minutes.

"Joel?" Lacy's voice was muffled behind the pink cloth she held to her face, protecting her eyes.

"What, Lacy?"

"Can you make me a braid when my bath is done?"

Without asking, he knew from where that idea had sprung. After leaving the tack shop, Megan's name had cropped up in everything Lacy had to say until she'd finally fallen asleep. What irritated him was the way he'd remembered Megan's dark hair and eyes exactly, when he tended to recall most women from that phase of his life from the neck down. Noncommittally, he told Lacy, "We'll see." He finished rinsing her hair, intending to get started on that tent.

But when he rose to his feet, Lacy sang out in protest. "That bird might fly in."

He couldn't blame her for being leery of staying in the house alone. "There's a screen on the window to keep out that bird. I'll just get your clean clothes from the truck and be right back."

Lacy seemed satisfied, already busy washing her doll's hair. Joel left her, grimacing as he stepped from the clean bathroom floor to the dusty hallway. Outside, the warm summer air seemed fresh in comparison to the stuffy house.

Joel crossed the gravel drive that was more dirt than gravel, opening the truck door and pulling Lacy's overnight bag from the floor. He riffled through a rainbow of little T-shirts and found Ted, the stuffed brown pony she slept with in lieu of the traditional bear. Searching for Lacy's jeans, he uncovered a silver-framed picture of Luann.

Reassured by the faint sound of Lacy singing from the house, Joel lifted the picture he had given to his daughter after the divorce. It was a glittery image, with a silver-studded saddle on Luann's palomino and silver sequins sprinkled over her shiny black outfit. A sparkling crown adorned her black hat. Lacy's mother. The queen of the rodeo.

He'd thought her beautiful once, with her golden hair and sapphire eyes. They'd seemed a perfect pair; the rodeo champion and the rodeo queen. In the wake of his father's death, her love had seemed to fill the void within him. Now he could only wonder how they had lasted those four years together.

Joel looked at the picture, searching for all he had once fallen in love with. But he saw only hardness and self-absorption in the depths of Luann's eyes. He remembered only a mother too busy to care for her child.

Joel laid the photograph aside. He wanted to provide a home for his daughter. But Megan wasn't making things easy for him.

Joel snapped the bag shut. He whirled when Lacy's scream split the sultry air.

Joel ran, gravel spitting from beneath his boots, another porch step giving way. He raced through the house. "Lacy!" He grasped the knob of the bathroom door and twisted. It was locked. "Lacy! Are you all right?"

"I can't get the door open, Joel."

She wasn't hurt. But Joel's knees weakened at the trembling in her voice. He jiggled the knob again, hoping the door was only stuck. "How did you lock the door, Lacy?"

"I used a key. I wanted my privacy."

Joel groaned. He remembered the talk they'd had about privacy. He also remembered the one they hadn't had about keys. "I want you to get the key and slide it under the door to me."

"I don't have it." Joel jumped as Lacy's voice echoed up from the register at his feet. "It fell into the hole in the floor."

With a sense of foreboding, Joel leaned down and peered through the keyhole. Lacy was looking into the bathroom register, her arms clutched across her chest, little rivers streaming from her wet hair and over her bare backside. His heart melted at the sight of goose bumps on her skin and her cold, curled toes.

"Daddy will get you out of there." Joel straightened. There was no way Lacy could lift the iron grate on the register. He looked at the heavy oak door, then at its hinges, wondering if his toolbox was still behind the truck seat. "I want you to wrap up in your towel while I get my tools, Lacy."

"The towels are way up high."

Joel cursed himself, remembering he'd set their towels on the shelf he'd wiped off. "Don't try to climb up. I'll have you out of there real quick, I promise."

He found the tools in the truck where he'd stashed them before leaving South Dakota. Joel hurried back to the house, comforting Lacy with his words until he realized he couldn't pry loose the painted-over bolts and hinges. He muttered an oath, wondering what to try next.

"Are you getting me out yet, Joel?"

Lacy sounded more demanding than upset now and Joel found that somehow reassuring. "You bet, Lacy." Knowing there was no way she could reach the high window, he told her, "I'm going to go outside and climb in the window. Then I'll get the key out of the register and unlock the door. That way, we won't have to take off the door and you can still have your privacy."

"I don't want my privacy. I want out!"

Joel winced, but he could hear Lacy's tears again and hastened to soothe her. "I know you do, Lacy. I'm going out to the window now."

Moments later, Joel stared bleakly at the narrow screen, watching the curtains flutter inside the bathroom, seeing the window was much smaller than he remembered. He could jump up and grasp the windowsill a couple of feet overhead. He just wasn't sure he could climb through it.

But he had to try. Joel pulled off his hat and turned to lay it over a nearby bush. In the distance, he spotted the deep blue shine of a pickup as it wound between cornfields on the ribbon of blacktop. A pickup the same midnight blue as the one parked in front of the Miller Tack Shop that morning. Joel caught a glimpse of dark hair and envisioned the almond eyes of Megan Miller.

Slender Megan.

Joel grimaced. Then, still clutching his hat, he ran toward the road.

* * *

Beyond the gently waving rows of cornstalks that were already waist-high, Megan could see the peaked roofs of two farmhouses. The second house, in the distance, was hers. The first was the home of Joel Crawford.

The summer breeze rushed in to soothe her like a country version of white noise. But it didn't help ease the tension knotting the back of her neck, didn't erase the crease from her forehead.

The moment Joel left her shop, she'd called her dad in Arizona. She'd gotten Suzanne, instead. It had taken a while to steer the conversation past Suzanne's excited, almost uncharacteristic nervousness about college, to the sale of the store. Her sister had finally informed her that Dad planned to call her soon. He was gone at the moment, getting an allergy shot in preparation for the visit home to meet with Joel.

It had struck her then that she had no choice but to continue working until Joel was ready to take over the store. Her father couldn't stay in Paradise without jeopardizing his health. Just coming back to sign the papers would be a strain for him.

Damn Joel Crawford. As his place came into view, Megan took a closer look at the farm, hoping it wasn't in as bad shape as she'd thought. The yard and surrounding pastures were mowed, but the sagging fence lines were choked with weeds. How long would it take Joel to repair them? Megan squinted down the lane, her heart sinking at the sight of boarded-up windows.

A flurry of motion at the side of the house caught her attention and Megan unconsciously slowed the truck. It was Joel, running toward the road, waving his straw hat to flag her down. Sunlight danced on the hat's turquoise feather and burnished Joel's tawny hair to gold. As he bounded to the edge of the road, Megan's grip on the steering wheel tightened. He stepped into the path of the truck and she cursed, hitting the brakes.

God, he had nerve! If he thought he could stop her on the road and harass her, he was in for a surprise. If she hadn't thought the truck might hit him, she'd have simply swerved around. At the moment, she wasn't feeling much inclined to tell him she'd be staying to work in the store.

Joel jogged to the side of the truck. As it rolled to a stop, he grasped the ledge of the door. Drawing a quick breath, he leaned close.

Before he could speak, Megan warned, "I don't have time for this now."

Joel let out his breath, dropping his hands from the door to stand looking down the road. Just when she thought he would walk off, he swung back, and Megan leaned away from his face. His eyes were like ice chips, his nostrils flaring. Color washed into his cheekbones beneath his smooth, tanned skin, a muscle clenching in his jaw. She couldn't drag her gaze away.

"Dammit, Megan, it's Lacy," Joel finally said through clenched teeth.

Megan's heart caught then, and she felt herself pale with dread. A sick sensation washed over her, reminiscent of the time Suzanne had fallen down the stairs and gotten a concussion.

"She's locked herself in the bathroom," Joel continued.

Locked in the bathroom. Megan closed her eyes in relief. In the space of a few seconds, she had imagined the worst. Unnerved by the fright he'd given her, she snapped, "Why didn't you say so?"

"You didn't give me a chance!" Joel reined his temper with visible effort. "Lacy dropped the key down the heat register and I can't get the damn door off. Between the two of us, I think we can get in the bathroom window—that is if you can spare a minute to help."

"Of course I can," Megan said, indignant, ignoring her initial reluctance to get involved in Joel's domestic problems, which she suspected were many.

"Pull in there." Joel pointed to the gravel drive, then stepped away. "I'd better get back to Lacy. I'll be on the far side of the house."

He jogged off and Megan parked her truck behind Joel's, the silver trailer alongside. As she switched off the engine, she spotted a bay horse in a nearby paddock, the gate held on by baling wire. Pushing her way out the door, Megan slammed it shut and headed around the house.

She found Joel staring up at the window, seemingly unaware of the sweat trickling down his temple. For the first time, she noticed his T-shirt was damp, clinging to his lean torso. He didn't spare her a look, just called out, "Lacy! Megan is here to help now."

"Hi, Megan. Please hurry."

The forlorn little words squeezed around Megan's heart, stirring instincts too strong to deny. She was suddenly glad she'd been driving by. Judging by the size of that window, Joel couldn't have gotten Lacy out on his own.

Joel positioned himself below the window. "I'll raise you to the sill." He measured her with a quick, thorough glance. "You ought to fit through okay."

Megan felt a reluctance of a different nature now, looking at the corded muscles of Joel's arms. Just being near him was enough to make her pulse sprint. To lift her, he might have to put his arms around her...have his hands on her.... Years ago, she might have died for the opportunity, but not anymore. Resenting the effect he had on her, Megan asked, "Don't you have a ladder?"

She had his full attention now. That muscle was working in his jaw again, his full lips pursing. Long heavy seconds passed before he spoke. "No. Now come on. I'll give you a leg up."

Joel laced his fingers together. Megan stared at his hands, still feeling the warm effects of his gaze. She slowly stepped forward, telling herself she could handle a little contact with Joel—a hand on his shoulder to steady herself a moment, that was all.

Megan raised her booted foot, her hands curling into fists. Her foot settled into the cradle he'd made and Joel gave her a sudden boost that had her grasping at his shoulders. Blue eyes flashed before her, then Megan was up, reaching out to catch hold of the windowsill.

"I've got it!" Even as the words left her mouth, Megan's foot slipped from Joel's linked hands. She caught herself, her hands dropping back to his shoulders as his arms came around her hips. Megan sucked in a breath when Joel turned his head, his silky hair brushing her bare belly beneath her cropped T-shirt.

"You okay?" Joel was looking up at her, his hot breath kissing her skin. Megan shivered, while perspiration beaded her forehead.

"I'm okay." Aware she sounded as if the air had been knocked from her lungs, Megan added firmly, "I can still reach the window. Just move a little to the left."

Joel moved and Megan raised her arm, catching her lip in consternation as her shirt rode higher. She reached for the windowsill, only to find herself flailing for balance when Joel stumbled back. His curse was muffled against her stomach, then his grip on her loosened. Megan slipped down, clutching at his neck. He took her with him as he fell, one arm tightening around her, the other cushioning her head as they hit the ground.

Winded, Megan sprawled beneath his heavy weight, feeling his hot breath fan her damp temple. Dry grass pricked at the tender flesh of her sides. One of her arms was trapped, her hand flattened to his chest, their legs a tangle of jeans and boots, knees and thighs. She should have felt uncomfortable. Instead, darts of pleasure arrowed through her.

Feeling Joel's belt buckle dig into her belly, Megan's heart began to pound. She shoved at his chest. "Get off of me!"

Joel levered his weight to the side. "Why the hell did you let go of the sill?" he rasped.

His eyes bore into hers. Megan swore she saw the burn of desire in them. Leaning away, she glared at him, suspicion forming in her mind as she remembered the way his weight had pressed into her.

Then she realized what he'd said.

"I did *not* let go of the window. I said move *left* and you—" Megan reached out and poked his hard chest "—moved *right*."

Ignoring the threat of her hand, Joel leaned close until there was no space, no air, between them. "Maybe we ought to run through that fall again. That way, you could get the facts straight."

"Joel! It's cold in here."

Joel sprang back and pushed to his feet in one swift move. Megan scrambled up, flustered, and frowning over both father and daughter.

"Coming, Lacy," Joel assured the child. "Look, Megan, Lacy is cold. Her hair is wet from her bath and she—"

"Lacy was in the tub?" Megan stared at Joel in disbelief, suddenly remembering her father's stern admonishment never to leave Suzanne alone in the tub. She'd been overwhelmed by the responsibility the first time he'd left them on their own, going back to work the fields until well past dark. "You left a four-year-old child alone in the bathtub?"

Joel's gaze narrowed. "Yeah. I did."

"Fool." Megan hadn't meant to speak the thought out loud. But as Joel's face took on a burn, she realized her folly. Still, the words didn't seem to stop, her voice rising as they spilled out. "*Anything* could have happened to that child. She could have gotten soap in her eyes. She could have slipped and struck her head. She could have *drowned.*"

Her words settled into a silence that gave them an air of hysteria. Megan felt her face color. What was the matter with her? She wasn't ten years old anymore. And Lacy wasn't her responsibility.

"I think we'd better concentrate on getting Lacy out," Joel warned.

Lifting her chin, Megan walked to the window. Joel came to stand beside her. This time when he cupped his hands, she planted her foot firmly in them, rising to grasp the windowsill. Giving the screen an upward shove, Megan hauled herself over the ledge, swinging inside.

Lacy sat on the edge of the tub, her arms hugging her middle, her eyes wide and uncertain.

Though Megan couldn't recall reaching out, seconds later Lacy was up and wrapped in her arms, burrowing against her in an effort to ward off the chill of the bath. Instinctively, Megan cuddled Lacy close.

Lacy's strong grip loosened. Megan found herself looking into the child's vibrant eyes as Lacy complained, "I was cold after my bath. But Joel said I can't climb up to get my towel."

Megan glanced at the high shelf Lacy indicated and suspected the daunting height had more to do with her not climbing after a towel than anything Joel might have said. Carrying Lacy over, Megan told her, "See if you can reach it now."

Lacy smiled and plucked her towel from the shelf. "Mine's the pink. Joel's is blue," she explained, clutching the towel to her chest.

Pinks and blues. The notion touched her somehow, drawing Megan's sympathy for father and child.

Carefully, Megan lowered Lacy to the floor. She didn't want to feel any sympathy for Joel. "Let's wrap this towel around you, then I'll get the key from the register."

Lacy was more than willing to be wrapped up, despite the warmth of the summer night. Satisfied the little girl was comfortable now, Megan knelt by the register.

"I can help." Lacy joined her. But when she looked down into the dark "hole," her eyes grew wide and she leaned close to Megan. "I think there's a spider down there."

Megan hesitated. The prospect held little appeal.

"Joel always gets the spiders for me," Lacy said.

But Joel was locked out. They shared a glance, two females about to brave the risk of spiders. Together, Megan and Lacy lifted the grate.

There were cobwebs but no spiders as Megan pulled out the narrow brass key. She and Lacy traded triumphant grins. Then a knock came at the door and Joel called, "Lacy? Megan?"

Lacy hopped up and ran over. "We got the key, Joel."

"Good girl."

Megan's smile faded. She looked at Lacy, who stood before the door, all wrapped in pink, tangled wet hair in need of brushing. An unexpected yearning filled her, but Megan pushed it aside. Joel would take care of his daughter now. Key in hand, Megan rose to unlock the door. When it swung open, Lacy stepped through like a regal princess, then leaped into Joel's arms.

Heedless of the wet strands, Joel laid his cheek against Lacy's hair, her bare white bottom resting on his strong tanned arm. A grudging gratitude glowed in his eyes. "Thanks," he said gruffly.

But Megan's attention had strayed from the tender picture of Joel cradling his daughter. Dismay swept through her at the sight of the cobwebs floating about his head. Dust filled her nose and she sneezed.

"Bless you," Lacy said, laughing.

Joel looked defensive. She'd been right about the house, but Megan was too shocked to gloat. She edged past Joel and Lacy, taking in the sheet-covered furniture with its coating of dust, her nose wrinkling over the mildewed braided rug. She stepped into the kitchen to her left, drawing up short at the sag in the hardwood floor.

"Lacy needs clothes." Joel headed out the kitchen door, not missing a stride when the top hinge broke free, leaving it to fall against the house. Lacy peeked over his shoulder with a grin as he crossed the small side porch, his long legs carrying them toward his truck.

Megan's sigh of despair was lost in the quiet of the house. With her boot, Megan pressed her weight onto a sagging board, and the floor echoed her groan. The chirp of a bird filtered through and she realized bleakly that the sound was coming from upstairs. She took a long look around. Judging by the work Joel had to do on his farm, she could be stuck in Paradise forever.

Drawn by the pound of a hammer, Megan stepped onto the porch. She stared in amazement.

Joel and Lacy were putting up a tent. Right there in the front yard, as if this were part of the Kampgrounds of America instead of a run-down Nebraska farm. Lacy was content to hammer at a stake, but Joel seemed determined to make quick work of getting the tent up. Megan had the feeling he was working off a bit of steam, over both the state of the farm and her.

Camping out was probably a treat for Lacy, just like any other kid. The little girl stopped hammering to yawn, and Megan could almost hear the soft sound, feel the warm breath. Lacy probably hadn't even had supper yet. Someone ought to be reading her a story, tucking her into bed. Like her mother.

Megan started to turn away, understanding Lacy's needs all too well. Just then, Joel straightened from tying down the tent, his legs unfolding with the lanky grace known to cowboys, the sweaty gray T-shirt riding the hem of his jeans at his hip. He pulled off his hat, swiping at his face with his forearm, pushing his hair into disarray. As he raised his arm to settle the hat back on his head, Megan watched the flex of sun-bronzed muscle, feeling like a girl again, pedaling by a field of hay and seeing only Joel.

If she fell this time, Megan thought, she would do more than skin her knees. Joel wasn't the reckless boy she'd once had a crush on. He was a divorcé, a father settling down to a life she was leaving behind. With a last bleak look, Megan propped the door shut and walked over to Joel and Lacy. She would give him the "good news" that she would be staying to run the store, then she would leave.

Lacy was busy spreading out the sleeping bags inside the tent. Megan stopped beside Joel, and couldn't help noticing the fatigue that shadowed his blue eyes. At that moment, Lacy crawled out of the tent, staining the knees of her clean jeans, her freshly brushed ponytail already mussed. "I want a cookie."

Joel lifted his tired, hungry daughter. Megan thought how he'd just driven from South Dakota. She doubted Joel had any kind of meal planned. He probably hadn't even been to the grocery store. On impulse, Megan reached out a hand and brushed the dirt from Lacy's knee. "I have a pot of chili at home. Why don't you and Lacy have supper at my place tonight?"

Lacy cheered an agreement, but Megan missed the little girl's grin as Joel's eyes darkened beneath his hat brim. She felt more than saw the warning there.

"Go get an apple from the truck, Lacy." Joel leaned down, pointing Lacy in the direction of his rig. The moment she was out of earshot, he turned to Megan, a hard look in his eyes. "We'll get our own supper, thanks."

She knew it was irrational to let his clipped words hurt her feelings. Joel was just letting his male pride stand in the way of what was best for Lacy. But her voice was unsteady as she told him, "You're being stubborn. Lacy needs to eat—"

"I know what my daughter needs. We get by just fine on our own."

Clearly, he meant to keep things that way. That suited her fine, Megan thought, her angry glance emcompassing the neglected house, the tent and Lacy crossing the yard with an apple in hand. She didn't want to get involved in all of this, and Joel had just handed her the perfect opportunity to make a clean escape. "Suit yourself," she said, trying to sound offhand. "Before I go, you should know I talked to Dad. I've agreed to run the store until you can take over, but—" her next point, she wanted to make clear "—only because Dad can't stay to do it himself."

"I'm glad that's settled."

"So am I."

Each knew where the other stood. But when Lacy came over to tug on his jeans and Joel hauled the child to his hip, Megan found it hard to take that step, to just turn and walk away.

She found it harder after her terse goodbye.

Lacy bucked in Joel's arms, boots and ponytail swinging as the little girl howled, "I want supper at Megan's!"

Chapter Three

"Lacy!" Exasperation thinned Joel's lips. His free hand caught hold of a little cowgirl boot, stopping it short of landing a debilitating blow. Megan flinched beneath the black look he sent her before reprimanding his daughter. "Mind your manners. Megan has to leave."

"But she said we can come for supper!"

Joel's gaze bore into Megan's. Her chin lifted, she told him, "The offer stands."

"I'll eat all of my food," Lacy promised, peering under Joel's hat brim.

Megan could see Joel struggling to hold his temper, his anger directed at her. He knew what would be best for Lacy. But she braced herself, waiting, aware she would be very disappointed if he didn't put Lacy before his pride.

"All right," he growled. "We'll go to Megan's. But we—"

"Let me down, Joel." Lacy wriggled and Joel let her slide down the length of him. She danced to Megan's side. "I want to ride in Megan's truck."

"That's fine with me." Megan grasped Lacy's hand, and, hoping to avoid another battle with those turbulent eyes, told Joel, "We'll meet you there."

"Hold on."

Megan waited, but her patience had neared its limit.

Apparently, Joel was tired of arguing, too. All he said was, "I'll be a few minutes behind. Lacy, you behave until I get there."

Megan wasted no time leaving, buckling Lacy in the pickup's passenger seat and backing out of the drive. As she headed down the road, she could almost feel Joel's brooding gaze upon her back. What had she been thinking, inviting him to supper? When they were young, she'd admired him, worshiped him from afar. Now everything about him seemed to rub her the wrong way. Megan released an impatient breath and immediately felt Lacy's scrutiny. She looked into the little girl's solemn blue eyes.

Her heart turned butter-soft. She knew what it was like to be little and to be aware of adults arguing. Lacy probably hadn't missed the tension between her and Joel, much as she would like to think so. She could remember being five, remember the way her parents had fought. She'd always known when they had argued, even if she hadn't heard them.

Curving her lips in a bright smile, Megan asked, "Do you like hot dogs with your chili?"

She'd said the magic word. Lacy loved hot dogs, and playing the truck's radio, and looking in the mirror behind the sun visor. By the time they turned in the driveway at Megan's house, Lacy seemed to feel right at home. Megan imagined the child was used to adjusting to new people and strange places after traveling the rodeo circuit.

Once inside, they checked on the chili Megan had left simmering in a slow cooker that morning. Lacy claimed to be starving, and Megan saw no sense in making the little girl wait to eat. After warming a hot dog and filling a dish with chili, Megan asked, "What would you like to drink?"

"We always have soda with chili," Lacy said, dipping her spoon in her bowl.

I'll bet you do. Frowning over Joel's notion of nutrition, Megan suggested, "How about some milk?"

"I like chocolate milk."

Megan was willing to compromise.

As she'd promised, Lacy ate every bite, chattering between mouthfuls. Megan smiled, only half listening, thinking how much she enjoyed Lacy's company in the quiet house.

Luann Crawford's name drew Megan back to attention.

"She's the queen of the rodeo," Lacy bragged.

"That's nice." But Megan felt no admiration for the "queen." How could Luann have walked out on Lacy when the child was only two?

And how could you have walked out on me and Suzanne, Mother?

Lacy set down her spoon. "My mother doesn't live with us anymore. She needed her space from me." The room filled with a silence that hurt Megan to hear. There'd been no telltale catch in Lacy's voice. But the quiet carried the sound of a little girl's pain. Of a guilt Megan recognized all too well.

As a child, she'd been convinced that her parents' arguments over her had led to their divorce. Her father had finally been able to explain the deeper complications, the differences in ideals and goals that had torn him and Patrice apart. But she would never forget the burden, the pain, of believing her parents' divorce was her fault. Neither would Lacy.

Clutching her dishes, Lacy climbed to her feet. She went to the sink, carefully rinsing the bowl and setting it on the counter.

"You're very good at that." Megan rose from her chair, trying to hide the anger that pulsed through her. She felt a sudden loathing for a woman she'd never met, unable to understand how Luann Crawford could deliberately burden a child as young as Lacy with so much guilt.

"I was my mom's helper." Lacy came to stand before Megan. "I know how to fold clothes and make beds, too. She showed me how."

Megan paused in the act of smoothing a hand over Lacy's hair. Joel stood at the kitchen door, watching through the screen. He'd showered, his hair dark gold with dampness, the sharp fresh scent of soap still clinging. The black T-shirt he wore emphasized his masculinity, yet he looked vulnerable, a puzzled expression on his face. And hurt. His eyes were clouded with it, as if Lacy's words had somehow wounded him. Lacy glanced up at her father like a child caught with both hands in the cookie jar, and a sense of misgiving ran through Megan.

"Lacy—" Joel seemed to struggle for words. Lacy had obviously lied about Luann, and Megan sensed his uncertainty over whether to correct her. Opening the door, he came inside and gently told her, "Daddy showed you how to do those things."

Lacy's small face reddened. She burst into tears and ran from the room. The front door banged a moment later.

"Lacy—" Joel stared after his daughter, his expression one of shock.

He didn't know, Megan thought. He didn't realize how Lacy was hurting.

From outside, they heard the truck door slam. Automatically, Joel patted his jeans pocket, and Megan heard the clink of keys. The sound was followed by his frustrated sigh. "I don't know what brought that on."

How could he be so blind? Curbing her impatience, Megan told him, "Lacy seems to miss her mother terribly."

Joel shifted, the movement restless, dismissive. "Lacy hasn't seen Luann since the divorce. It's for the best. It does Lacy more harm than good when we run into her."

His eyes had narrowed, as if he replayed a distasteful scene in his mind. The lack of passion for his ex-wife was understandable, but the denial she saw worried Megan. How could he help Lacy if he couldn't accept that his daughter missed Luann? Her own father had reassured her and Suzanne, but he had been helpless to ease the pain of their mother's departure. Patrice had left and had never been heard from again. But Joel knew where Lacy's

mother was. He could at least make the effort to let
Lacy see Luann.

"Don't look at me like that." Joel had raised his
gaze to hers, and his eyes flashed in defense. "I
don't criticize Luann for Lacy to hear. I don't have
to. Lacy learned firsthand about her mother."

Megan stared at Joel in disbelief. Did he really
believe Lacy didn't care that Luann was gone? That
she didn't hope every day that her mother would
come back? "Lacy called her mother the queen of
the rodeo. That's how she sees Luann."

Joel snorted, his disgust evident. "Luann left
her. Abandoned her."

"Lacy blames herself for that."

"No." The denial was as flat as the look in his
eyes. "Lacy was there when her mother walked out.
I'd better go see to her now."

He turned, pushing his way out the door, his
back a rigid testimony to his stubborn words. The
door slammed and Megan's defeated sigh settled
into the quiet. Her heart went out to Lacy and, before she could stop the feeling, to Joel. But he
wouldn't want her sympathy over what she thought
must have been a terrible scene.

The kitchen was suddenly too confining. Megan
went out the door and saw Joel in the truck, holding his daughter. Lacy was exhausted. Certain Joel
would leave as soon as the child settled down, Megan turned the other way, going out to the fence to

whistle the horse, Molly, up from the pasture. To make the trip worthwhile for the old mare, she went into the barn and scooped grain from the bin. By the time Megan walked out, Molly was shuffling to a halt beside the wooden feeder. Megan stroked the mare's neck as if the coarse white hair was silk, ignoring the prominent veins that belied Molly's age.

Molly was a constant in her life. The Taylors, who'd leased the crop land and planned to buy the farm, had promised to look after Molly. Megan smoothed Molly's thick forelock while the mare methodically chewed. Lacy would like Molly, she thought. The mare was gentle and patient. Tolerant.

Propping a boot on the bottom rail of the fence, Megan folded her forearms on the top board and rested her chin on her hands. She'd like to photograph Lacy with Molly. A contrast of young and old. Lacy's bright golden hair and Molly's dull white coat. She could almost see Molly tiredly lip apples from Lacy's small hand, while the child's face lit with delight. Molly's age would be telling in sunlight, while Lacy would seem to blossom.

Dry grass rustled from behind her. As she listened to Joel's boot steps close in, Megan felt tension rising within her. Part of it she was resigned to. Despite her better judgment, she was drawn to Lacy, her mind churning to find a way to help the child cope, to make Joel see what Lacy suffered. But there was more.

Joel stopped behind Megan. Her heart was suddenly beating just as hard as when she'd sprawled beneath him outside his bathroom window. Harder. Megan fought the swarm of sensations that made her muscles want to go slack and her knees weaken, then she turned to face him.

He was closer than she expected. Her gaze skated up his chest to his smooth jaw and finely shaped lips, finally meeting his eyes. The tension coiled unbearably within her.

"Lacy's in the truck. She cried herself to sleep. I think I'd better take her home now," he said. But he didn't move, staring at her, a frown marring his smooth forehead. Beneath the thick wheat hair that fell across his forehead, his skin was a shade lighter where his hat protected him from the sun. He seemed kind of undressed without that hat.

Joel inched closer. "I want you to know that I realize you have Lacy's best interest in mind. I haven't forgotten that your parents are divorced, too."

Megan's gaze dropped to Joel's shirtfront. She used to imagine her mother marching into school to pluck her from class, much the way Stephanie Winthrop's mother had every time Stephanie went to the dentist to have those braces checked. Only in her daydream, her mother had been taking her

home and they were all going to be together
again....

"What I'm trying to say," Joel continued, "is
that Lacy and I are pretty used to the way things
are now. I don't want you to—I'd rather you
didn't—"

"Interfere?" Joel's struggle for words drew Megan sharply into the conversation. Indignation
warmed her face.

"If that's how you want to say it." Joel's eyes lit
with a gleam that dropped ten years from his appearance. His slow perusal made her blood heat in
her veins. "You've grown up, Megan."

The irreverent thought crossed her mind that she
wished she could show him just how much. But
then, she thought wryly, her innocence would
hardly impress him. He'd want a woman who knew
how to please a man.

But the way he was looking at her, the appraisal,
the speculation in his eyes, had all kinds of possibilities coming to mind. She would know what to
do. Know what she wanted him to do.

Joel's hand came up slowly, sliding into her hair.
As his fingers threaded themselves in her braid,
Megan's breath suspended in her chest. She fervently wished she'd already changed her "look" for
something more sophisticated. Sexier. Instead, she
was dressed the way his daughter had been, her
sticky bangs springing from her forehead where

she'd shoved them with her fingers. She saw hesitation flash in Joel's eyes. Yet it seemed he was going to kiss her, anyway.

He closed the distance almost unwillingly, his hand tensing at the back of her head, his eyes dark with inner conflict. Megan folded her hands in tentative fists against his chest, but, ignoring the turmoil she saw in Joel's gaze and ignoring her own late-blooming voice of reason, she lowered her lashes and raised her chin. This kiss wasn't in her plans, but it had once been something she'd dreamed of. One kiss couldn't hurt....

But it did. With the touch of his lips, all the yearnings and unfulfilled dreams she'd tucked away when Joel left town came painfully to heart and mind once again. Megan's hands uncurled, flattening on his soft cotton T-shirt, the hard muscle beneath bringing back the long-ago memory of his bare, bronzed chest. Relishing the feel of his arm tightening around her, Megan poured all of her stored-up emotions into the deepening kiss, hoping to stir some heated memory of herself within him.

Suddenly, Joel's hands gripped her upper arms. He pushed her back to lean on the fence, his fingers tightening, as if to keep her there. "I was right. You have grown up."

He seemed almost wary of her, as if she'd seduced him against his will. A thrill swept through her to think her kiss had affected him so. But he looked so determined not to let it happen again that anger replaced the tingle inside her. *He* had kissed her. Letting him was her only mistake.

Shrugging off his hands, she told him, "That's right. I'm not a child. I don't play games."

His jaw tightened with her warning. But he only muttered, "That's probably best for all of us."

Joel stalked away and Megan blinked back the hurt stinging her eyes. It had felt so right when he'd kissed her. Now everything felt wrong.

Because it *was* wrong. Joel knew it, and it was best that she face the fact, too. She planned to leave Paradise and it was clear that Joel intended to go things alone with his daughter. Whatever had triggered that kiss had best be ignored.

Megan waited until Joel had driven away, then walked to the house. The sight of the empty plates reminded her Joel hadn't eaten. Well, as he'd said, they did just fine on their own.

Not hungry, Megan wandered into the living room. The magazine Suzanne had sent poked out of the straw bag Megan carried to the store each day. Maybe she'd look it over, experiment with her hair and some makeup. Giving herself an air of sophistication was probably going to take more time than establishing herself as a photographer. But all her efforts would be worthwhile once she'd found her mother and Patrice saw the change in her, the success she had become.

For tonight, she hoped her efforts would help erase the sight of Lacy's tear-filled eyes and the feel of Joel's mouth on hers.

Claire Evanston. Joel lifted the hot fudge sundae she slid through the little screened window, unable to believe that the woman he'd spent his adolescence in love with still ran the ice-cream parlor. Even now, pushing fifty, Claire still had an air about her, not to mention the same red hair.

Joel handed down the sundae to Lacy. "Tell Claire thank you." He waited until she had done so, then pointed her in the direction of the tree-shaded picnic table where they had sat for lunch. When Lacy had safely deposited the ice cream on the table and sat perched on her knees on a bench, Joel turned and looked up at Claire.

There were lines fanning Claire's green eyes, gentling a sultriness he'd once coveted. Lines he knew represented the hard life of a woman who'd raised a daughter alone. "You look great, Claire," he told her, and meant it.

"I look fifty, but then you always were a sweet boy, Joel. I never expected to see you back this way again, let alone with a daughter."

"It wasn't something I expected either." There'd been a time when he couldn't put small town life behind him fast enough in his quest for a trophy buckle. Joel hooked an arm on the counter, turning to look at Lacy who sat spooning fudge like a waterfall over her sundae. Lacy had come along as a surprise, one he'd learned to cherish, one Luann had never accepted. "Things have a way of changing."

Claire patted his ringless hand, understanding all too well. "Lacy's a fine little girl. I guess she'll be going to school here since you're buying the Miller Tack Shop."

Joel gave a wry grin. Nothing was secret in a town the size of Paradise. "I hope to buy the store."

"Matt and his youngest girl moved to Arizona. I guess you know his oldest daughter, Megan, is running the shop."

"I'm counting on her to keep on working a while. I need to get settled in at the farm. But she's got some notion to go to California and take pictures."

"She's really quite talented, you know. She took some pictures of my granddaughter. They were remarkable."

"I guess I can understand her wanting to leave. But now I'm having second thoughts, knowing I'd have to take over right away. You'd think she'd want to help out for her father's sake."

Claire sobered. "That girl's already done a lot for her father's sake and her sister's, too. That family had it rough until Matt got the store going about seven years ago. The girls were still pretty young when his wife left them. If I remember right, they never heard from Patrice Miller again."

Joel remembered Megan always having her little sister in tow and he thought how their clothes had had a faded look about them. But Megan's dark hair had glistened in a fascinatingly long slash of braid down her back and her eyes had shone beneath a fringe of black lashes.

"Why don't I get us some coffee?" Claire offered. "You can tell me more about Lacy."

"Sounds good."

Joel went to sit on the bench across from Lacy. She was stirring her sundae into chocolate milk, a good sign that she was finished with her treat. What was she thinking? Joel wondered. Lacy seemed content as a kitten with a bowl of cream. Until last night, he would have taken for granted that she was. Now he couldn't help worrying that she was thinking of Luann.

Joel laid his hat on the table, letting a hot gust sift through his hair. His gaze followed the path of the breeze up the street. He could just make out the Miller Tack Shop sign, swinging sassily in the late day sun. The anger that had kept him tossing and turning all night churned anew within him.

Megan had planted the doubt in his mind and it had taken root, enough that he couldn't sleep. Enough to set a fear gnawing inside him that maybe Megan was right. Despite all the pain Luann had inflicted, maybe Lacy still missed her mother.

"Can I go swing?" Lacy stood at his side giving him a sweet, chocolate-rimmed smile.

Joel brushed at her mouth with a napkin. "You'll have to ask Claire. It's her swing set."

Claire set two cups of coffee on the table, then ruffled Lacy's bangs. "You're welcome to play on it."

Lacy ran off, calling a thank-you over her shoulder, the braid she'd insisted upon swinging across her back.

"Pretty hair," Claire murmured, looking after Lacy.

"She got that from her mother." Joel sipped the hot bitter coffee and wished for a cigarette.

"With Connie, it's her eyes. Dark like her daddy's instead of green like mine."

A quiet understanding passed between them. Joel sensed an acceptance in Claire that he hoped he'd come to know one day. He looked over at Lacy, lying across a swing on her belly, her braid hanging over her shoulder, and murmured, "I think maybe Lacy's been missing her mother."

Claire sighed, apparently aware of the circumstances of Joel's divorce. "I wish I could tell you it gets easier. But it hurts, watching a child grow to think that a parent doesn't want her.''

They sat in silence a moment, Claire sighing over the past, Joel worrying over the future. What if he failed his daughter again? Unlike Megan, he hadn't been able to see how Lacy was hurting.

Under other circumstances, he realized it might have been good for Lacy to get to know Megan. But his daughter's obvious adoration of the woman worried him. The bottom line was, Megan was leaving. Lacy didn't need that kind of hurt again.

Neither did he.

Chapter Four

Three days later, Joel pulled out of the drive, Tally in tow in the four-horse trailer. It had been over two weeks since Belle Fourche, time spent healing for Tally. Joel glanced down at Lacy, sitting beside him, wearing her pink straw hat. They were ready to rodeo.

Morning had dawned bright and warm beneath a clear sky that promised the day would only get hotter. Burwell was only an hour or so away and would be an easy haul for both them and the horse. But first, he had to swing by the tack shop for his saddle.

He'd avoided Megan these past few days, trying to put that kiss out of his mind and waiting for word from Matt. He'd also wrestled with his conscience, recalling the way he'd told Megan not to interfere where Lacy was concerned. He still felt it would be wrong to let Lacy get too attached to Megan, but Megan had opened his eyes to Lacy's feelings about Luann. He'd come to the conclusion that an apology was the least he owed her.

Lacy had worn a long face over not seeing Megan, making him feel guiltier than he already did. She'd cheered up some when he told her once the house was fixed up, she could invite Claire's granddaughter to spend the night. He couldn't imagine himself chaperoning a slumber party, but Lacy's happy face had convinced him he was going to have to give it a try.

First he had to get that house cleaned up. Not really sure how to go about it, he figured he'd just tackle one room at a time. He already had them sleeping inside, even if it was in the kitchen.

Reaching the edge of town, Joel pulled into Bill's Stop and Go to gas up the truck. He checked the oil and purchased a breakfast of sorts inside the station's small store, then drove down the road to the tack shop. Megan's truck was parked outside, along with another flashy red pickup.

Inside, a tall, dark-haired cowboy was shooting Megan a winsome smile as he hefted a box of supplies from the counter. "Sure I can't talk you into that movie, honey?"

Joel paused in the process of closing the door, meeting Megan's gaze from beyond the cowboy's shoulder. Her eyes flickered, a wariness coming into them that made him feel like a heel and doubled his pulse rate all at once. But he didn't back down. That cowboy was all but leering at her, at her dark hair hanging around her shoulders, at the lime-colored tank top skimming the round tops of her breasts. She had no business getting mixed up with that kind.

Megan's gaze skittered back to the dark-haired cowboy. "Maybe some other time."

"Anytime, babe," he said, grinning. Box in hand, he swung toward the door, sidestepping Lacy and passing through as Joel held it open.

Joel watched the cowboy swagger off. The man walked like a bronc rider, rolling a little, reminding him of the guy Luann had left him for—originally, anyway. Strong cologne hung in the air and stung his nostrils. The guy even smelled the same.

Maybe some other time.

Joel let the door bang shut. The other night, Megan's kiss had seemed fresh and innocent, making him think she'd been locked away in her daddy's store too long. Now he wondered if maybe his judgment might be off and Megan was more experienced than he thought. After all, she must be twenty-five, even if she didn't look it.

Turning around, he found Megan talking over the counter with Lacy. She looked at the beef jerky in Lacy's hand, and back at him.

Joel grimaced at the "ever hear of eggs and juice?" look in Megan's eyes. Reminding himself that he'd planned to apologize, and aware Megan had a point, Joel swallowed his resentment and walked over, plucking the jerky from Lacy's fingers. He tossed it in a small trash basket. "You shouldn't be eating in the store, Lacy. You can have an apple when we get in the truck." Before she could throw herself like a sulky filly, he sent her to look for a bottle of liniment. Lacy dashed off, eager to prove she could read the label.

"Have you heard from Dad?"

Joel looked into Megan's eyes. They appeared almost sultry beneath her thick lashes and he noticed her lips were glossed a pale, lush pink. The flowery scent that drifted up to him was subtle, almost teasingly so. He wondered where she'd dabbed it on, then realized she was waiting for an answer. He let out a breath. "Not yet. Have you talked with him?"

"No."

In the silence that followed, they seemed to come to the same conclusion that it was best to let that subject lie.

Megan licked her lips, making them shine. "So what can I do for you?"

He could think of a lot of things. Herding his thoughts in the right direction, Joel told her, "I need my saddle, if it's finished." He had newer, fancier saddles he could use, but the old Circle Y was his favorite, broken in like a comfortable leather chair.

"It's right over here."

Megan came from behind the counter and Joel felt his mouth go dry. The slim denim skirt she wore revealed long, firm, lightly tanned legs and, when she turned her back to him, the sweetest curve of derriere he'd ever seen. She bent, about to lift his saddle from where she'd propped it near the others on display, and Joel said, more sharply than he'd intended, "I'll get that."

Megan straightened, wide-eyed. "Suit yourself."

Joel hauled the saddle near the counter, turning to watch Megan as she walked over. He couldn't remember ever seeing her in anything but jeans or shorts, even during his senior year in high school when she'd been a freshman there. He'd noticed her, anyway, but if she'd dressed like this back then, he'd probably have done more than just look.

She fidgeted uncomfortably and Joel realized he was staring. He didn't want her classifying him with that other cowboy and lightened the look with a smile. "You look real pretty today, Megan."

Her surprise was disarmingly unaffected. She smoothed her skirt self-consciously, her voice coming a little fast and breathless. "Thanks. I'm working my way up to something more sophisticated for my trip to California."

Joel didn't want to talk about California.

"This was as close as I could get without feeling silly," Megan went on. Her soft laugh was self-deprecating as she added, "No one would mistake me for Suzanne."

Joel told himself to drop it, but found himself prodding, "Your sister?"

"Yes. Suzanne is smart, a real brain, but she's also gorgeous and knows all about fashion." Megan's voice was at once envious and wistful.

Joel felt his heart melt a little. Megan didn't even know how pretty she was. And she didn't seem to take into account the years she'd given to her father and sister. "I'd say her sister probably gave her a push in the right direction."

She held nothing back with her smile, the first real smile she'd given him, and with it, she seemed to knock the air from his lungs. If she had smiled at him like that years ago, instead of shooting him shy glances, Matt Miller would have had to chase him off with a gun. But she waved his answer aside. "Suzanne was *always* perfect, even as a child. I was the one always getting into trouble. Mom called Suzanne 'princess' and me a tomboy. I wasn't anything like my mom...."

Her voice trailed off, her face flushing with embarrassment, as if she'd revealed more than she had intended. That vulnerable look made him want to set her at ease, but Lacy came running up to his side, thrusting a bottle of liniment to the countertop. "Here's the 'sorbine, Joel."

Megan went back behind the counter and Joel watched her ring up the charge. She avoided his gaze and Joel held his tongue, feeling he'd already gotten in deeper than he wanted.

Lacy seemed to have no such reservations, informing Megan, "This is for our horse, Tally. We're taking him to the rodeo."

"Over in Burwell," Joel felt compelled to supply. From outside in the trailer, the horse gave a confirming whinny.

Megan's eyes seemed to flicker in surprise. Joel handed her a bill and noticed a tiny frown line form, disappearing beneath the fringe of her bangs.

"Anything wrong?" he asked. Her gaze slid to Lacy, then she shook her head, laying his change on the counter.

"No. Nothing," she said curtly, irritating him to no end.

"Megan—" Joel caught himself, and leaned down to give Lacy the change. "Get us some gum for the road, will you, Lacy?'' When she'd gone, he turned back to Megan and suffered another disapproving glance. Now what? No gum before noon? With raised eyebrows, he gave Megan another chance to unload.

"It's awfully hot today," she said pointedly, giving the words an emphasis that left him to guess their hidden meaning.

For the life of him, he couldn't. "Yeah. It's hot." After a lengthy pause that tried his patience, he added, "So?"

"It's just—never mind."

Joel released a long breath. "Never mind what?"

"It's just so hot." She fidgeted. "Lacy will burn in the sun."

"I'll see to it that doesn't happen." Joel cocked his head. "That it?" Judging by her glare, it wasn't.

"It's going to be nearly a hundred degrees today. And who will watch Lacy while you compete?"

Joel shifted, impatient. "Lacy's always chatting up the cowboys and pestering the cowgirls. There's usually someone around the chutes willing to give her a ringside seat on their horse."

"*Usually?*" Megan muttered, shaking her head again. "You can't really mean to take her to the rodeo all day in this heat."

"What the hell else am I supposed to do with her?"

"I can stay here with Megan."

Joel shot a swift look at Lacy, startled to find her standing at his knee.

She popped a piece of gum into her mouth. "I can stay with Megan like you let me stay with your friend Mary."

Megan's dark eyes flashed and Joel groaned. He could almost see her mind working, trying him and finding him guilty of letting Lacy stay with a string of women "friends." "Mary's the wife of my friend Todd," he hastened to tell her, then gritted his teeth for explaining when she continued to glare at him. "Lacy, Megan has to work. And you have to go with me."

"But I want to stay here." Lacy turned up her face, her little bow mouth starting to tremble, her eyes glistening beneath the pink hat brim. "I want to stay with you," she appealed to Megan.

"Lacy." Joel reached down and picked up his daughter, trying to fight the punched-in-the-gut feeling he always got when Lacy cried.

"I'll be good," Lacy implored, and it suddenly seemed her blue eyes were too much for Megan to resist.

"Let her stay."

Lacy blinked back tears and smiled. Joel gave Megan a long look, tightening his hold on his little girl. He'd just spent three days trying to explain to Lacy that Megan would be leaving soon, trying to temper her enthusiasm for Megan before she got carried away. Spending the day with Megan didn't seem in keeping.

"I'll take good care of her," Megan said huffily, as if she thought that was the reason for his hesitancy.

Joel knew Megan would take good care of his daughter. She clearly thought his methods of parenting could use some improvement.

The heat of the day burned through the shop's windows behind him. For a moment, Joel let himself imagine what it would be like for himself and for Lacy, if he let her stay. He remembered the countless times he'd deposited her in the saddle with someone he barely knew while he took his turn in the box. Remembered the way she'd fall asleep with her head on his shoulder as they made their way in the dead of the night to the next town, the next motel, the next rodeo.

Lacy squirmed and Joel let her down, watching as she ran behind the counter, striking a pose similar to Megan's. Joel sighed. He'd already warned Lacy that Megan was leaving. Surely things wouldn't get out of hand in óne day.

He glanced at Megan. Some time with his daughter might open her eyes a little. Her perfect little sister wouldn't have prepared her for the likes of Lacy. He couldn't help warning her, "Lacy can be a handful."

"I'm sure we'll get along fine."

"I should be back around dark," Joel said, relenting and thinking she wouldn't sound so smug after a day of chasing his daughter.

"You can pick Lacy up at my place."

"I appreciate this." Joel called Lacy over for a quick kiss, admonishing her to behave. Megan joined them in front of the counter. Joel picked up the bottle of liniment. "Guess I'd better be going."

"Well, good luck."

"Thanks. I can do with some." Joel hefted the saddle and walked to the door, then remembered the apology he'd meant to give Megan. Turning back, he saw her and Lacy, crouched down to examine the contents in the display case. Megan's little skirt was hiked tantalizingly high and he almost groaned aloud.

Megan caught him watching. Her eyebrows rose and she tipped her head, her dark hair swinging, completely oblivious to the havoc she caused within him. "What?"

Joel thought of the hassles Megan had put him through since the moment he'd walked in. He shook his head and elbowed his way out the door. "Never mind."

He was miles down the road, fighting a craving for a cigarette and trying to banish the vision of a leggy Megan before he realized he'd forgotten to leave Ted with Lacy. The fuzzy brown pony blinked up at him from the seat, and he suddenly noticed how lonely it was without Lacy chattering or snuggling up to sleep beside him. Lacy would miss Ted if she started getting tired, but he figured Megan was up to handling the situation. Joel turned on the radio, unwilling to question his trust in Megan where Lacy was concerned.

The day was as hot as Megan had warned. Joel liked knowing Lacy was out of the heat. There were a few familiar faces, and he knew he would have gotten by if Lacy had been with him, but it was nice not having to "get by" for a change. His mind was on his work and it showed in the flawless sail of his loop and the dexterity with which he threw his calf, neatly catching up three of its legs with two wraps and a half hitch. His time of 9.9 seconds wasn't his fastest, but it was enough to win the calf roping.

Several cowboys came by and prodded him to join them for a beer in celebration, an indulgence he was seldom able to enjoy with Lacy to consider. Joel stowed his gear in the trailer, the sun burning through the cotton of his white shirt, sweat gathering beneath the band of his hat. A cold beer would taste damn good.

His gaze swept the familiar scene of cowboys, dust and milling stock. Without Lacy along, or close friends like Todd and Mary, his success today felt a bit hollow. His thoughts turned to Megan, and Joel slammed the trailer door. Maybe a couple of beers with the boys would banish this empty feeling inside him. As an added attraction, a few "buckle bunnies" had been asked to join the party. Joel saw the invitation in one of the women's eyes and gave the cowboys a nod.

It was well past twilight when he pulled through Paradise. The town seemed to have settled behind closed doors, yellow lamps glowing through drawn shades. The neon lights of the ice-cream parlor were the only sign of life in town. But he'd already had too much partying. With a toot of the horn for Claire, Joel followed the road out of town. He stopped at his own place long enough to bed Tally down for the night and unhitch the trailer, then he headed to Megan's.

He was glad he'd sobered up with time and coffee before driving home. All that remained was this warm, kind of fuzzy feeling that had him alternately wanting to whistle or grin. He didn't even want a cigarette. Joel glanced at his reflection in the rearview mirror and winced at his lopsided smile. Long as he didn't grin, Megan would never know he'd been drinking. He didn't want her to spoil this good mood with one of her disapproving glares.

Not when she looked so damn pretty when she smiled.

Megan had looked soft and appealing today, not at all like the women he'd seen at the rodeo, with their painted-up faces and lacquered hair. The beer he'd drunk had been cold and had gone down fine, but he was glad he'd passed on the women.

Joel turned into the gravel driveway at the Millers' small, two-story farmhouse. He lifted off his hat and dropped it on the truck seat, fingers combing his hair. Welcoming light poured from an open window and spilled over the porch, and Joel took a moment to enjoy the sense of home fires burning, of Lacy safe and secure, of someone waiting for him after he'd spent a day on the road. Then, careful not to slam the truck door, he climbed out and walked up to the porch. His step slowed at the top of the short row of stairs.

Through the sheer curtain that hung over the window, he could see Lacy and Megan curled together on a small sofa bed, while the flickering lights of the television danced over their sleeping forms. His daughter's arm was flung over Megan's waist, some small fuzzy toy clutched in her hand. But it was Megan who drew his gaze, her dark hair spilled over a pale pillow. The navy T-shirt she wore was enticing, reaching just to her bare knees and molding to the gentle rise and fall of her breasts.

Long seconds passed before Joel rapped on the window frame. Megan jerked awake. Carefully moving Lacy's arm as the child slept on, she slid off the mattress. Joel stepped back to wait, tucking his hands into his back pockets.

A moment later, Megan pushed open the screen door. She blinked up at him, weaving a hand through her hair, the wide neck of her shirt drooping to bare the opposite shoulder. "I'm sorry. I didn't mean to fall asleep."

And Joel didn't mean to stare, but he couldn't seem to help it. Her dusky hair fell free, brushing delicate collarbones and framing a face flushed with sleep. She looked soft and warm and so naturally pretty that it was all he could do not to touch his hand to her cheek. Her long slender legs tapered to small bare feet, and he entertained the notion that there was nothing but Megan beneath the dark T-shirt. The outline of a pair of shorts dispelled part of the image, but the lack of a strap at her shoulder was enough to stir a vision of creamy, rose-tipped breasts.

"How did the rodeo go?" Megan's voice was still husky with sleep and every bit as seductive as the picture in his mind.

"I won the calf roping." He found himself waiting for her reaction.

"So that's what kept you," she said, smiling. "Did you compete in any other events?"

"I just rope now. The year I won the All-Round title, I partnered up with Todd and team-roped, too." Because she really seemed to be listening, he reminisced, "When I first started out, I did anything and everything. Bareback or saddle-bronc riding, steer wrestling. And there were always the bulls." Joel grinned, remembering the aches, the pains, the thrills. He remembered the way the girls looked afterward, all wide-eyed, the way Megan was looking at him now.

"You were pretty competitive back then."

"Reckless," he corrected, having learned the difference.

"More like *rest*less. You were different than other kids your age. Older, somehow."

He'd felt older than his peers back then. But right now, he felt pretty good. He grinned down at her teasingly. "You were always dragging your little sister around or riding that blue bike."

Her face grew pink.

"One time, you fell by my mailbox, where the ditch is deep."

The pink in her cheeks became a bright blush. "I remember. You were out in the hay field. I hoped you hadn't seen how clumsy I was."

So, she'd been watching him, as well. Joel let his grin widen. "I was looking at your legs. I worried that you'd skinned your pretty knees."

He'd caught hell for it, too, when the bales he'd stacked had fallen. His father had had him re-stacking them long after she'd ridden out of sight.

Megan was laughing now, her hands pressed to her cheeks. He realized her smile was somehow connected to that warm feeling inside him, for it had intensified the moment her lips curved. Probably, her good mood was only the result of being half-asleep. But he liked to think her feelings stemmed from just being here, in the moonlight, talking with him.

Megan straightened her shirt, shooting him a look of self-consciousness, and he realized he was staring again and wearing that silly grin. "So, did Lacy behave herself?"

"She was fine. She missed her pony, Ted, but I had an old bear she could sleep with."

Gratitude welled up within him, carried on an intense wave of awareness he'd tried, but failed, to deny. It was time to go now, before all these feelings inside him made it impossible to leave. "Thanks for watching over her, Megan. I'll get Lacy and head on home."

"Wait." Megan came a step closer and Joel felt the heat of her body waft over him, through him. "Let her sleep. Tomorrow is Sunday. The store isn't open until afternoon. I can drop Lacy by on my way in."

"There's no need for that."

"But she's sleeping so peacefully. Unless you think it would upset her not to go home, there's no reason to wake her."

"She won't be upset." Lacy would love it, Joel thought wryly, knowing that was the problem. He really ought to risk Megan's disapproval and explain that after spending her young life sleeping in motels and pickups, and even dozing occasionally on the back of a horse, a blast of dynamite wouldn't wake Lacy once she'd fallen asleep. He ought to take his daughter home.

"Let her stay. She needs her rest," Megan insisted.

Judging by her straitlaced ways, Megan had probably had his daughter in bed since eight o'clock. Lacy would be up at the crack of dawn for sure. He guessed it might as well be Megan making Lacy's breakfast as him. "Okay. But I'll come by for her in the morning."

"Don't go without giving me Ted this time," Megan reminded him.

Joel stepped from the porch with reluctance. "I'll be right back."

She'd moved down the steps when he returned from the truck. The stars burned a halo around Megan's head, a faint breeze stirring her hair against her cheek. The very thought of leaving brought back that hollow feeling he'd had at the rodeo. Just as she'd triggered the warmth inside him, Megan was the cause and the cure for this emptiness within him.

Joel let his hand linger to touch hers when he handed her the pony. Her skin felt soft beneath his callused fingers and the scent of her rushed up to him like some kind of sweet night flower. She'd grown very still, and he knew she didn't want to draw away from the magic any more than he did. It was all the encouragement he needed.

Catching her wrist, he slid his hand gently, but purposefully upward, his thumb grazing the smooth skin of her inner arm, his palm cupping her shoulder, his fingers slipping into her hair. The thick strands spilled over his forearm, a silky web he had no desire to escape. Megan held the look of longing, her tongue moistening her lips in unconscious invitation. There was a potent innocence about her, a sweetness he couldn't resist.

Lowering his head, Joel touched his lips to hers and watched her lashes flutter down.

Megan trembled beneath her navy shirt, no more able to stop her lips from parting than stop the earth from spinning. He drew her closer, the slight pressure of his hand at the back of her neck bringing her head to nestle in the warm crook of his arm. Her breasts settled against his chest with a rightness that quelled the whisper of reason in her head, that banished any thought of pulling away or holding back.

His arm tightened around her waist. Megan's hands skimmed over his taut sides, her palms seeking the sleek hard muscles of his back. She relished the heady feeling of being pressed to his long, lean body. His hair brushed silkily at her temple when he slanted his mouth to trail kisses along her jaw. Megan sought his mouth again, hungry for him, for the tangy, somewhat bitter flavor.

Megan stiffened. Her mind registered fully the taste of him, the flavor and the scent of beer. No wonder he'd been so mellow, so appealing tonight. No wonder he'd kissed her. Megan snatched her arms from around him, ignoring his surprised sputter. When he would have reeled her back in, she jerked away, heat washing into her cheeks. "You've been drinking."

"I had a few beers." Joel straightened, giving her a disgruntled frown. She couldn't detect a sign of slurred speech or lack of balance but...

"That's why you were late." She could easily picture him, hanging out with his buddies, corraled by admiring cowgirls. Had he been kissing one of those women, too? "I imagine you find it funny, my kissing you, not realizing—"

"I'm not drunk, Megan."

"Are you going to tell me now that you *haven't* been drinking?"

Joel shook his head, his eyes brightening. A chuckle escaped him. "You sound like somebody's wife."

Megan's breast heaved with indignation. She hadn't been kissing the wild young boy of her dreams this time, she'd been kissing the man he had become—or thought he had become. And all he could do was laugh at her. Hot spots of anger burned beneath her cheeks. "In this case, I'm glad I'm not. Thank God you left Lacy with me. You had no business on the road. You're probably lucky you made it home."

The humor had vanished from his eyes with her tirade. "I've got a lot of problems, but drinking isn't one of them."

And though he did indeed seem suddenly very sober, she snapped, "It would seem that tonight it is."

Before she could avoid him, Joel moved in, leaning close, his warm breath whisking across the cheek he'd just kissed. "It didn't seem to bother you a minute ago."

Megan stood rooted, her face burning with the truth of it. She ought to slap him, walk away. But the hot, shivery feeling his nearness sent rippling through her was too fascinating, too compelling to break free of. She could see the pull of it sweep over him, as well. He was going to kiss her again....

A shout burst through the window.

Lacy. Megan jumped and turned toward the stairs, but Joel's hand on her arm stopped her. They both looked toward the window.

Inside, Lacy muttered and slept on.

The night air wafted over Megan's hot cheeks and her bare toes curled in the cool damp grass. She was achingly aware of Joel's hand on her arm and the fact that she still wanted his kiss. She made herself step back, and Joel's thumb moved gently over her skin before he let go, leaving her to wonder if he felt the same sense of confusion over these feelings that coursed between them.

She knew at least one thought ran the same through their minds. Lacy didn't need the complication of an attraction that was purely physical, that would only bring more upset to her life.

Even knowing this to be true, it hurt to hear Joel say it.

"I'm sorry, Megan. I didn't mean for this to happen." He dragged a hand through his hair, the age-old gesture of frustration as timeless as the ache that wrapped around Megan's heart. "I've been dragging Lacy from one rodeo to another since she was born. Bad as the situation was, it didn't get any easier after Luann left. Lacy deserves better and I'm trying to give her that. But I have to be careful. I don't want to see her hurt again."

"I don't, either." Megan mustered as much dignity as she could. "As long as we both agree on that, we should be able to get along until I leave."

Megan wondered at the frown that fleetingly crossed Joel's face. Then he seemed to accept what was. "I'd better go."

But first, he bent to scoop Ted from the ground where the pony had fallen, lost during the embrace.

He handed the pony to Megan, their fingers brushing and drawing away quickly, the small stuffed toy a symbolic reminder of Lacy, sleeping just beyond the open window.

Chapter Five

Megan lifted the lid on the cedar chest. Morning sunlight streamed through a front-room window, brightening the faded patterns of the winter quilts she'd stored, lighting the deep corners of the chest. "This is where I got the bear you slept with last night, Lacy. My sister has a doll in here you can play with. Somewhere."

It was beneath the layers of quilts, in a protective box. A birthday present, the doll was the last gift Suzanne had received from their mother. Suzanne had always taken good care of her toys, but this doll was like new. Perfect.

Megan thought of the ragged bear she'd given Lacy to sleep with last night, the only salvageable toy she owned. How many times had her mother scolded her for dragging it around everywhere she went?

It had surprised her, the way Joel seemed to understand Lacy's need to carry around Ted. Of course, in Joel's case, it was more likely a matter of following the path of least resistance. Judging by the pony's dingy state, Joel certainly wasn't overly worried where cleanliness was concerned.

"Did you find that doll yet?"

Megan looked over her shoulder at Lacy. "I've got it." She took the doll out of the box. "Here you go. She smells kind of funny from being in the chest, but that will wear off, just like it wore off of Bear."

Lacy seemed entranced by the blue-eyed doll in a velvet dress. "What's her name?"

"She doesn't have one. She belonged to my sister. Suzanne didn't really play with the doll, just kept it on a shelf. I don't think Suzanne will mind if we take her out if we're careful with her. Maybe you can give her a name."

"I'll call her Princess. When Joel tucks me in at night, he calls me Princess."

Funny, Megan mused, how easily she could imagine Joel's big, callused hands tucking a blanket around his daughter while he called her Princess in his husky cowboy drawl.

"You got any more toys in there?" Lacy peered into the cedar chest.

"No, there was just this doll and old Bear. I'm afraid Bear's not quite as perfect as that doll." Megan sighed, thinking how the bear and the doll so aptly represented her and Suzanne.

"That's okay. I like this bear. He's smiling." Lacy smiled back at the bear. "When I have my birthday, my mom will probably get me one."

"When is your birthday, Lacy?"

"In August. My mom will give me lots of presents then."

Megan had her doubts about that. She watched Lacy cuddle the bear, wishing there was some way to cushion the little girl from the hurt the future held in store. "Would you like some orange juice to drink while you play?"

Lacy nodded and yawned simultaneously. With the doll hugged in one arm and the bear in the other, she climbed onto the rocking chair where she'd set her toy pony. When Megan returned with the juice moments later, Lacy was curled in the chair, sleeping soundly.

Small wonder. The child had been up since six. Megan imagined it was a novelty for Lacy to spend a quiet day inside. They had gone out just long enough to feed Molly and for Megan to snap the pictures she'd wanted. She'd give a copy of the best one to Joel and Lacy before she left for California. Megan touched the little girl's hair, then reminded herself there were dishes to wash.

At ten-thirty, the telephone rang. With dripping hands, Megan snatched the receiver off the hook, wondering if it might be Joel, then deciding he was either still sleeping or nursing a headache—although she'd spent a restless night debating just how drunk he'd actually been. Peering around the kitchen corner, she satisfied herself that Lacy was still asleep and murmured, "Hello?"

"Megan?"

"Dad!" She'd been piqued by the way he and Joel had made plans without consulting her, but as her father's lean, handsome face came to mind, he was forgiven, her sense of longing outweighing all else. She felt like a little girl again, watching him head out to the field, knowing he wouldn't be back until nightfall. She missed him. She missed Suzanne.

"Speak up, Meg. I can't hear you."

Megan turned back into the kitchen, settling into a chair. "I didn't want to wake Lacy."

"Lacy—Crawford?"

"She spent the night here."

"Well. I guess you and Joel have gotten acquainted, then. I take it he's told you he's buying the store?"

"Yes. He also told me I was going to be working for him." She wasn't above making her father squirm a little.

"I know, and I'm sorry, Megan. Joel was going to be in a tight spot, trying to move back onto the farm and take over the shop all at once. Enough that the promise of your help seemed to sway the deal. I'd really appreciate your doing this while I get a new store opened."

Megan immediately felt guilty. Her dad had worked hard for her and Suzanne, trying to be a good father and make a success of the store. She'd waited fifteen years to be able to leave. She could wait a couple months more. "Don't worry, Dad. I don't mind working if it will help sell the store."

"Things are looking pretty good here for getting another shop open."

As her father launched into the details, a shuffle at the kitchen doorway drew Megan's gaze. Lacy wandered over, small knuckles rubbing her eyes, one hand clutching the tattered bear. Without hesitation, she climbed onto Megan's lap, resting her head against Megan's shoulder. She was still warm and relaxed from sleep and Megan hugged the little girl, touched by Lacy's trust and affection.

Enjoying the cuddling, Megan reminded herself that a lap was a lap to Lacy. The child certainly hadn't minded being left here for the night. She thought of the woman, Mary, and wondered how many other women had been a part of Lacy's life, if they had all been married friends of Joel's.

"Megan?"

"Sorry, Dad. Lacy just woke up." It seemed natural to give Lacy another squeeze.

"Sounds like you and Joel are getting along pretty well."

Megan thought of the past few days, the tension and arguments, the kisses. She looked down at Lacy's sleep-flushed cheeks. So much emotion in so little time. "We get along okay," she lied.

"I take it Joel was gone somewhere last night?" Her father suddenly sounded the way he used to when she, or more often Suzanne, had a date.

"He was at a rodeo. He won the calf-roping event."

"Is that so?"

Her father's speculative chuckle was enough to trigger heat in her cheeks. Furious with her reaction, Megan changed the subject. "Dad, are you still coming back next week?"

"I'm not sure."

"You're not feeling worse, are you?"

"I'm fine."

"Is Suzanne there? Can I talk to her?"

"She's out shopping now."

Megan laughed. "I hope you can make it next week. I miss you and Suzanne."

"We miss you, too, sweetheart. Maybe you can get out here sometime and see the new house. Suzanne wants to show you where she'll go to college this fall and I should settle the deal on the building for the new store soon."

"I'd like that, Dad. I could stop there on my way to California."

Her father was silent for long moments. "You're still determined to go?"

"Of course. I—" *Have to.* "I've planned this for a long time."

"I know you have." Matt sighed. "Megan, are you sure that this...career is what you really want?"

Megan clutched the receiver, frowning. She'd thought that particular lecture over when she'd had her first picture published in a children's magazine. Her dad had encouraged her then. But lately, he seemed to be raising all the old doubts again. "I'm sure, Dad. California is where the rich and famous are. If I want to see my work published in *Personality Magazine,* that's where I have to go."

Lacy wriggled off her lap, Megan's glance following the child to the door and meeting Joel's intent stare through the screen. Her heart rippled through its beat. Instead of hung over, he looked fresh and full of masculine vitality this morning, his turquoise shirt seeming to lend its color to his eyes. She couldn't help thinking how handsome he was, a thought she'd carried for years and apparently hadn't gotten over. Before she could catch herself, Megan knew her response shone in her eyes.

Lacy opened the door and Joel bent to kiss the top of his daughter's head. Megan let her breath seep out and said quickly into the phone, "Dad, Joel's here now. I'll put him on." Wordlessly, she handed over the receiver.

Megan decided he needed some privacy. With a crook of her finger, she led Lacy outside.

Lacy soon abandoned Bear, whom she'd carried along, at the picnic table, to run across the yard and play on the tire swing that hung from a sprawling elm. Lacy's manner was uninhibited, distracting Megan from the murmur of Joel's voice drifting through the screen. The toes of Lacy's boots churned up miniature clouds of dust as she wound the swing round and round, finally raising her feet to let it spin.

When it stopped, Lacy sat looking dizzily into the treetops. Megan saw the child's gaze settle on a low fork in the tree. She could almost see Lacy's busy little mind at work, plotting a way up to that cozy nook. Megan smiled. Lacy was every bit the tomboy she herself had been. She used to hide away in that tree whenever she could.

Remembering the climb she'd once made to "save" her kitten, Megan's smile faded. She'd been wearing her white party dress, trying so hard to keep it clean for Suzanne's birthday celebration, trying so hard to please her mother. But when she'd heard Mouser yowling from the tree, she had no choice but to go to her kitten's rescue. The dress had gotten torn and soiled and Patrice had been furious.

Lacy had climbed from the swing and stood at the base of the tree, one small hand touching the coarse bark, her head tilted back in contemplation. Would Lacy succumb to temptation and reach out to a low branch? If Joel was outside, Megan had no doubt he would boost Lacy up at the first request.

Joel pushed open the screen door, stirring her from her musings. Lacy hopped back on the swing and ignored him, and Megan realized the little girl didn't want to leave.

Keeping the picnic table between them, Joel stopped, his hands shoved in his jeans pockets, looking at Lacy. Megan sensed his reserve, unable to stem the regret that followed. They'd come to an agreement last night, and it was obvious he meant to stick by it. She did, too. She just wished it was somehow easier.

"Matt sounded good. He said he'd call us both Wednesday to let us know if he'd make it back before the weekend."

"Fine." Megan glanced at Lacy. If Joel could so easily dismiss last night's kiss, she could, too. She had something more important on her mind, anyway. "I understand Lacy's birthday is coming up soon."

"The middle of next month. She'll be five." The words came on a sigh, as if Joel had wondered how it had already come to be.

"Lacy was talking about it this morning. She said her mother would be giving her lots of presents."

"And knowing the situation, you didn't think that was likely." Joel looked suddenly, utterly weary. He sank onto the opposite bench, lifting off his hat and laying it on the table. "You were right. The only reason she expects anything at all is because I gave her a *present* from Luann last year. Her mother never even called her, though I'd made sure Luann had the number of the motel we were staying at."

Megan frowned, but not over Luann. "You bought Lacy a present and told her it was from her mother?"

He straightened a little. "Yeah. I did."

"She's bound to find out the truth about her mother, sooner or later."

"I know that." Joel looked over at Lacy, his expression pained. "Scarcely a day goes by that I don't give thought to the fact that Lacy will someday realize that her mother doesn't want her. Never did."

Her father had never spoken ill of her mother, but he had never pretended the situation was anything but what it was, either. Softly, Megan asked Joel, "What happens when she realizes you deceived her?"

Joel's piercing gaze was filled with conviction. "What I did, I did for Lacy's sake. If it was your child, you would have done the same."

Megan frowned, uncertain, watching Lacy twirl in the swing. Suzanne's ponytail used to billow out the same way as Lacy's when Megan would push the tire for her. Suzanne had loved her ponytail, always wanting a hair band or ribbon to match her shirt. Megan could clearly recall the day Patrice had refused to buy striped ribbons for Suzanne, claiming they were too gaudy. Megan had sneaked back into the store and bought them for Suzanne with a coveted half-dollar.

Maybe Joel was right. Maybe she would have done the same as him and bought the present.

"I appreciate your taking care of Lacy." Joel had risen and was placing his hat back on his head. "That wasn't my intention when I came in the shop yesterday."

"I know that. And I didn't mind watching her. I like having her around."

Joel glanced away. "I'm glad, but I don't think she ought to stay with you again."

Megan stared at Joel, affronted. Last night, they'd each decided that Lacy's needs came first. Joel had trusted her enough to leave his daughter with her, even after that kiss.

That kiss. Embarrassment warred with indignation. What did he think she was going to do? Throw herself at him every time he brought Lacy by? Megan rose, facing him across the table. "I think I can control myself in your presence, if that's what you're worried about."

"That's not it." Joel pushed back his hat, clearly exasperated. "Telling Lacy you like having her around would make her . . . would just . . ."

"Just what? Make her feel loved? Make her happy?"

"Make her want you to stay!" Joel rounded on Megan, his hands coming to rest squarely before her on the table. Lowering his voice with visible effort, he demanded, "Don't you have any idea how much she thinks of you?"

Megan caught her lip. Hadn't she just noted moments ago that the child didn't want to leave?

That was a normal reaction for any child, Megan tried to reason. But she couldn't deny that she felt something special for Lacy, and sensed the little girl's feelings for her were special, as well.

For that same reason, she couldn't just turn her back on Lacy's needs. She met Joel's glare with determination. "I wouldn't do anything, say anything, to mislead or hurt Lacy. I'm willing to watch her when you rodeo—unless you prefer to drag her around in the heat, leave her in the hands of strangers while you rope—''

"Dammit, Megan." Joel's eyes burned with frustration, then he released a defeated breath. Megan knew she'd made her point. She caught Lacy's glance and stood, calling the little girl over.

"Lacy, it's time to go home."

Lacy swung sullenly a moment, then scuffed her way across the yard, her lip thrust out in a pout Megan was coming to recognize. Ignoring both adults, Lacy snatched Bear from the table and looked into his face. Then she told them, "Bear doesn't want me to go."

"He probably doesn't want to go back in that chest," Megan observed. She looked squarely at Joel, then said, "I'll leave him out and you can come back and play with him next time your dad needs someone to watch over you."

Joel shifted and Megan tensed, but he said nothing.

Lacy gave a satisfied nod. "Bear wouldn't want back in that box."

Megan had to agree. Her mother had taken Bear and locked him in the chest when Megan was nine, claiming she was too old for such nonsense. Megan had never lost the childish impression that Bear had hated it in that box. She'd taken Bear back out soon after her mother left home. It had been a good many years before she'd put him away again. "Why don't you take Bear inside and get your pony?"

"I'll be waiting in the truck, Lacy," Joel called, watching his daughter skip to the house. When he rested an icy gaze on her, Megan raised her chin, and turned the words he'd spoken earlier back on him.

"This has nothing to do with you or me. What I'm doing, I'm doing for Lacy's sake." With that, Megan walked up to the house to help Lacy gather her things.

The feeling that she'd somehow gained the upper hand lasted only as long as it took Joel to wheel his truck onto the road. She knew he was right. It wouldn't do for Lacy to become too attached to her, not when Megan would be leaving. She caught herself watching after Joel until he'd driven from view and knew she'd be wise to watch out for her heart also.

Even knowing that, Megan found herself spending that afternoon, plus the next two days, looking out the tack shop's window for Joel's truck, wondering if he would come by. In the evenings, on her way home from work, she took note of the progress he made with the fencing, her mood brightening if Lacy happened to be out playing and waved to her. She didn't see Joel, but found it easy to picture him in her mind, shirtless, his torso gleaming beneath the sun's rays as he bent to his task.

Megan tried to tune her thoughts back to her photography, her career, only to find herself in the darkroom her father had set up in the basement, developing the roll of film she'd used to take Lacy's picture. When she finally traded amber light for the sixty-watt bulb overhead, she turned to examine the negatives she had hung to dry.

Light and dark were reversed, making a black ribbon of Lacy's ponytail and turning the ghost-colored Molly into a shadow of a horse. But Megan saw past the distortion and knew she had captured Molly's patience and Lacy's joy. Her gaze returned to the negative she would make two prints of. One for Joel and one for herself. A lonely ache wound through her and she sighed, wondering how she had come to feel this way in the room where she had once treasured solitude.

The mood persisted until the next afternoon at the shop when her father telephoned with the news that he and Suzanne would be in town Friday and stay the night. As the cloud around her lifted, Megan promised, "I'll make your favorite, a pot roast, for dinner. And chocolate cake for Suzanne."

Her father chuckled. "That sounds great, but actually, Megan, I've already made dinner plans for all of us at the Circle R."

Megan raised her eyebrows. The Circle R was a dude ranch a few miles out of town that also boasted a fine restaurant, famous for its steak. "Shouldn't you wait until the shop is sold before you celebrate?"

"I'm hoping dinner will help cinch the deal. Never knew a cowboy who didn't like a good steak."

Megan sagged against the counter, his words seeming to steal her strength away. "You're inviting Joel to dinner?"

"And his daughter. Don't worry, we won't get carried away talking business. I expect we'll settle the details Saturday morning and sign the papers then. I just thought it would be nice to visit, too. I used to see Joel, Sr., in town sometimes. He was pretty proud of that boy."

"Yes, of course." Megan pressed a hand to her warm cheek, appalled at the thoughts that had just run through her mind. She and Joel at the Circle R with its low intimate lighting, small dance floor and slow, romantic music. How silly. That wasn't her scene, anyway. She'd always been more suited to high school basketball games, when she'd had the time to bother. "That's a nice idea, Dad."

"Well, it will be if I can get through to Joel. I tried to phone him all morning, but the phone is either out of order or off the hook. Maybe you could keep trying or stop by and tell him about dinner."

"I can do that," Megan said. They decided on reservations at seven o'clock Friday night, and after her father promised to give Suzanne a hug, Megan disconnected and tried to phone Joel.

There was only the same busy signal her father had mentioned and Megan returned the receiver to its cradle, a frown forming as she puzzled over the reason why. Maybe the phone hadn't been properly hung up after Joel's last call. Maybe Lacy had bumped it while playing. More troublesome was the image of Lacy alone, trying to use the phone because Joel was outside, hurt from a fall from his horse or some other kind of injury.

Megan caught herself then and tried to slow her overactive imagination. She wasn't going to give in to the urge to close the shop an hour early just to check on Joel. Megan sat at her desk a moment, staring at the account she'd been working on. Then she lifted her keys. She might not allow herself to check on Joel, but she simply couldn't sit here, thinking of Lacy, without worrying that something might be wrong.

Despite the blast of the air conditioner to fight the ninety-plus heat, her once-crisp white shirt clung limply to her skin and her jeans felt heavy by the time Megan reached Joel's farm. She rolled her pickup into the drive, raising dust and causing a flurry among the pigeons that had ventured from their roost in the barn. Megan cut the engine and climbed out.

Quiet enveloped her, only the faintest of breezes stirring the trees and the filmy curtains in the farmhouse windows. When no one came out of the house, Megan moved toward the barn.

The black truck was parked in front of the open double door. Crossing the yard, Megan saw no sign of Joel. She hesitated, standing in the sparse grass at the edge of the drive. The horse was no longer in the makeshift paddock. Maybe Joel and Lacy were out riding and the phone was simply off the hook. Maybe she should just leave.

The sun was still hot, and Megan felt needles of heat prickle her skin like a current. Like the way it felt when someone was watching you. Her face heated on a wave of self-consciousness. Megan took a step back, then stilled, her gaze drawn upward. Joel stood framed in the hayloft door, watching her.

His hands were curled around the twine of a heavy-looking bale. His red shirt hung free of his jeans and she could see the muscles bunch in his arms below the sleeves, see the stubborn set of his jaw below the shadow cast by the brim of his hat. His eyes she could feel. They bored through her, made her feel she wasn't welcome here.

But God, it was hard to look away, hard to ignore the pull of sun pouring over golden skin, of
red cotton stretched taut over wide shoulders. A
thick layer of sun-bleached hair curved around
Joel's neck, the light strands shining like silver
against his bronzed skin.

The bale dropped with a heavy thunk into the bed
of the truck. Megan started, her thoughts scatter-
ing. Joel jumped from the loft, shirttail flapping.
He landed atop the bale, then took a short hop to
the ground. Megan stayed where she was, her heart
jumping as he walked over, slapping at the dust on
his jeans. He didn't push back his hat in a welcoming gesture, just left her to peer under its brim and
read the stern question in his eyes.

Megan pushed a hand through her sweat-sticky
bangs. He was standing too close; she could smell
the clinging hay and feel the warmth emanate from
his body. The same nervous, fluttery feeling she
used to get whenever he passed by in the halls at
school went shimmying down her spine. For a moment, words escaped her. She felt foolish now over
the way she had worried. Then she remembered she
had a mission in coming here. Her voice stiff, she
told him, "Dad tried to phone you today. He wants
you and Lacy to join him—us—for dinner at seven
Friday night, out at the Circle R."

He took a long moment to think it over, and
Megan wondered if the tension between them might

cause him to refuse. Then he nodded. "That'd be fine. You say Matt tried to call?"

"All morning. He kept getting a busy signal."

"If my phone's out of order, I may have to use yours to report it. Let's go find Lacy and we'll see."

Find Lacy? He sounded as unconcerned as if he'd dropped a coin out of his pocket. Megan skirted the barn on his heels, thinking her father would have skinned her if she'd lost track of Suzanne when her sister was Lacy's age.

They rounded the corner and Megan heard Lacy singing. She missed a step, certain she had to be hearing wrong.

"Forty-eight bottles of beer on the wall, forty-eight bottles of beer..."

Obviously, Lacy had been singing for some time. Megan stared in disbelief at the little girl hanging over the pasture fence, carrots sticking out of each pocket as she entertained the bay horse dozing in the shade of a nearby cottonwood. Was this how Joel taught his daughter to count?

"Forty-six bottles of beer on the wall..."

"Lacy." Joel's cheeks had taken on the customary tint he wore when dealing with his daughter. "Megan is here."

Lacy twisted around and Megan caught a glimpse of a yellow braid swinging across the little girl's back. Wondering if Lacy had requested the braid, wanting to be like her, Megan was suddenly glad she'd abandoned her attempts at sophistication to-day and braided her hair in deference to the heat.

"Megan! Come and see Tally." Lacy's smile was infectious. Megan slipped past Joel to join Lacy at the fence. "Isn't he pretty?"

The horse had taken a roll in the dust, but beneath the thin layer of Nebraska soil, Megan caught flashes of gleaming hide. Considering this horse was worth more than her pickup, "pretty" didn't seem to do him justice. But Lacy was waiting and Megan didn't disappoint the little girl. "He's beautiful."

Pleased, Lacy turned to her dad. "Tally wants to see Megan."

Indulging his daughter, Joel came over to the fence and gave a shrill whistle. The bay lifted its head. Another whistle had the horse walking over. Megan admired the gelding's smooth, swinging stride, thinking the horse somehow suited the man beside her. She wondered if cowboys and their horses were something like pet owners with their dogs and cats, taking on one another's personalities.

"Tally's a roping horse," Lacy said proudly. "And Joel's a rodeo champion."

Then, before Joel could stop her, Lacy reached out and lifted his shirt, exposing the silver trophy buckle lying against the flat expanse of his stomach.

Megan couldn't help the tiny catch of her breath. Beneath the red cotton, Joel's bare belly was sunned as brown as his arms, laced with fine tawny hair that edged below the waist of his jeans. His skin looked like warm, slick satin. Megan's hands curled in reflex.

"Sorry." Joel pulled down his shirt and Megan watched its slow descent, half in relief, half in regret. Her gaze floated upward and met the knowing gleam in Joel's eyes. In that moment, he didn't look sorry at all. Then he grew impatient.

"We'd better go check on that phone." He turned toward the house.

Megan stared after him, trying to gather thoughts that had scattered. She started when Lacy jumped from the fence, eyes wide.

"Ted's on the phone."

It took a moment, Lacy's words sinking in as the little girl raced past Joel. Chuckling, Megan followed them, but her laughter caught in her throat as Lacy suddenly went sprawling in the drive. She ran over, but Joel was already scooping Lacy into his arms.

For a moment, he held her against his chest. Megan met his gaze over the little girl's head and saw the very real fear in his eyes. Then he pushed strands of hair from Lacy's tear-streaked face. Lacy choked back a sob and pointed to her knee.

"You're okay, Princess. Those Peter Pan bandages we bought will fix you right up."

"I want Megan to come," Lacy said, sobbing.

"She is." Joel shot Megan a quick glance that dared her to say no.

As if she would. Patting Lacy's leg, she reassured the child. "You can show me those new bandages."

When she stepped into the kitchen, Megan couldn't help noticing that Joel's progress inside the house was coming along at a much slower rate than outside. Obviously, building fence had higher priority than running a vacuum.

Joel perched Lacy on the kitchen counter beside the sink. Lacy's lower lip trembled, but it was mutinous now, her blue eyes tracking every move when Joel took bandages and Merthiolate from a cupboard off to his right. Megan winced at the thought of the sting it was sure to give as she watched from just inside the door.

Megan inched closer, unable to fault Joel's tender ministrations as he gently washed Lacy's scrape. Then he reached for the Merthiolate.

"I don't want that dammit med-cine," Lacy warned.

"You have to let me put on medicine, Lacy. You'll get an infection if you don't. And stop swearing."

"But I don't like it," Lacy sniffed, and teardrops spilled over her cheeks again. Megan stepped forward. Surely Joel had some kind of salve in that cupboard.

"Lacy, I'll be very careful. Daddy doesn't want to hurt you. Just let me put a little bit of medicine on and you can have that Peter Pan bandage."

"No!" Lacy cried. Her legs kicked in a flurry, her feet beating the drawers below.

"Lacy—" Joel fumbled with the bottle of Merthiolate, trying to still Lacy and dodge the rubber soles of the little girl's tennis shoes. A high kick sent the bottle spinning across the counter.

Megan leaped to catch it. Joel dived for it, too. His body pinned her to the counter and his hand clamped over hers—too late. Lacy stopped howling to watch the bright pink liquid pool on the counter just out of their reach. A stillness settled over the room, but Joel could feel the tension humming between his hand and Megan's beneath it.

This was what he had meant to avoid. But his arm was twined with hers and he couldn't seem to stop his gaze from following the satiny path of her skin upward. A turn of his head brought her face breathtakingly close. Dark lashes fluttered delicately, and her lips parted. Her breast was soft against his arm and he could feel the rise and fall of each shallow breath she took. He couldn't seem to breathe at all.

Lacy tried to squirm off the counter. Abruptly, Joel let loose of Megan, planting a staying hand on his daughter. With his free hand, he lifted his hat and tossed it on the table. His voice was taut as he told Lacy, "I want you to apologize to Megan for making a scene."

"No." Megan's eyes flashed. "Lacy was right. That's going to sting if you put it on her knee."

Joel gave her a quelling look. But she only turned her back and began sorting through the cupboard, drawing out a tin of salve. She came to stand beside Lacy, moving him aside with a "look" of her own. Joel stepped out of the way, fighting a sudden urge to pin her against that counter again.

But as Megan spoke to his daughter, the feeling changed. Her voice was sweet and reassuring, something Lacy had never known with Luann. It made him want to return her gentleness with a soft touch of his own.

"I'm going to put some of this salve on your bandage, then stick it over your knee," Megan crooned to Lacy. "Okay?"

Lacy nodded, sitting quietly while Megan washed her hands and not giving so much as a whimper when the bandage was applied. The two traded smiles, then Lacy looked to him for approval. "I was good, wasn't I, Joel?"

"The best." Joel lifted Lacy off the counter, planting a kiss atop her head. "Why don't you go throw the rest of your carrots to Tally?"

Lacy was off like a shot, the sore knee forgotten. Silence fell over the room like a heavy curtain. Megan faced the counter, and he noted her hand shook while putting the lid back on the tin. He told himself not to, then stepped closer, reaching out to help, taking the touch he craved. His palm settled over the smooth top of her hand and he felt her warmth move through him, feeding the need that burned inside him.

In no time at all, he knew that one touch wasn't enough. Megan stood very still, but he could feel the give in her, the softening of her hand beneath his. He turned her palm to his, then he turned her in his arms.

She wouldn't look at him. Joel raised a thumb to her cheek, grazing it, thinking it felt like the petal of a flower. "You look like—" His hand stilled. "Like one of those dolls a person can look at but never touch."

His words drew a smile. "A perfect doll, the kind that comes in a protective box?"

"Exactly." He lowered his hand, fighting a desire he recognized from long ago. "You've always been untouchable, Megan. Too young. Too innocent." Feeling her tremble, he suspected she still was.

"I'm not a doll," she whispered, her face turned up now, her eyes glistening.

He couldn't resist. Joel lowered his head and took her mouth gently, the way he might have done years ago when he was eighteen and she was fifteen. As the sweetness poured over him, the years fell away. He kissed the girl Megan had once been. Then he pulled her body against his and kissed the woman she had become.

Small steps pounded a warning on the back porch. Joel set Megan aside, steadying her until Lacy slammed open the door. He saw immediately that his daughter was too excited to notice Megan's flushed face or his uneven breathing.

"Joel! Can Megan stay and see my new bed and curtains?"

"She can stay." He said it without thinking. The way he'd done everything since he'd first touched Megan's hand. But he didn't want her to go.

"Will you, Megan?" Lacy pleaded.

She gazed down at Lacy, uncertainty clouding her eyes, then she said faintly, "I'll stay."

Lacy whooped and Joel let out the breath he hadn't realized he'd held. Lacy caught Megan's hand and his gaze trailed them out of the room, his heart catching at the sight of Megan's dark head bent to Lacy's blond as they shared some secret. When he headed out to work on the fence, he carried the image with him.

Chapter Six

Hammer in hand, Joel paused in his work for what seemed the hundredth time to listen to the sound of feminine voices drifting from Lacy's open bedroom windows; Lacy's girlish giggle and Megan's low, soft laugh. Squinting against the sun's bright rays, he thought of how much Lacy had missed out on, even before Luann had left. Thought of how much he enjoyed the sound of a woman's laughter...Megan's laughter.

Dropping the hammer, Joel tugged at the snaps on his shirt and dragged it off, letting it fall to the ground. He was eager to finish the section of fence, finding little satisfaction in working alone, fighting the pull of laughter from inside the house.

A short time later, with the sun creeping low in the sky and the heat of the day lessening, Joel set aside his tools. Pulling on his shirt, he walked to the house, head cocked toward the busy chatter still coming from upstairs. He wondered what Lacy and Megan had been up to all this time.

As he moved through the house, Joel noticed the phone in the hall was on the hook, with the pony, Ted, lying alongside. He stopped and lifted the receiver, the familiar buzz assuring him the phone was working. It didn't take much figuring to realize the phone had been off the hook. Ted had been known to make calls before. With a wry grin, Joel headed up the stairs.

He stopped at the threshold of Lacy's room, a little amazed by all Megan had done with soap and water. The wide windows gleamed and the ruffled curtains Lacy had chosen were washed and hung, a matching pink coverlet spread over her new bed. The hardwood floor now had a glossy sheen and the fuzzy pink rug he'd bought looked especially feminine tucked up to the little white dresser with its oval mirror. He felt big and suddenly awkward in the dainty-looking room.

But it was worth it, seeing the glow on Lacy's face. Her very own room. Even now, she was arranging toys in her closet, setting her dolls on her bed.

Megan turned from where she was placing clothes in the dresser, looking every bit as pleased, if a little more frazzled. Her white shirt was untucked and smudged with dust, her hair lacing her cheeks where the strands had pulled loose from her braid. But with her delicate features and her smile shining in her eyes, he couldn't help noticing the feminine setting seemed to suit her.

"This looks pretty good, ladies." Joel leaned in the doorway, his gaze resting on Megan. "But I think it's time to call it quits. It's getting late."

"We're not done yet, Joel," Lacy protested. "Megan said the rest of the floors need mopping and the bathroom needs cleaning and those saddles in your bedroom should be out in the barn."

"Is that so?" Joel watched Megan's face redden over Lacy's obvious quote while he easily pictured her in his bedroom.

"The new cleaning supplies were stacked in your room," Megan muttered, looking at her boots.

"Next to my saddles," Joel confirmed.

Her chin lifted. "Yes. Next to those saddles that belong in the barn."

Joel chuckled. Megan might blush easily, but she was no wilting flower. "That's where they'll be as soon as I get a tack room built."

"Lacy says you have a rodeo coming up soon," Megan mentioned, brushing at her jeans, her effort to change the subject transparent.

"In Kearny," Joel obliged. "I'm going to try to make as many rodeos as I can before I get those horses in and Lacy starts school."

"Kearny's quite a haul from here. Lacy's welcome to stay with me." Megan glanced at him then, and the look in her eyes warmed the resistance from his heart.

Joel looked down at Lacy, who was suddenly busy with her shoelaces, following Megan's cue to keep quiet, he suspected. Then the little girl peeked up at him, giving her sweetest grin, and the corners of his mouth lifted. "Yeah, I guess that would be a good idea. Thanks."

Lacy cheered and ran over and Joel caught her up in a hug. He swung her back down and she was off again, calling, "I've got to tell Ted."

The light thump of Lacy's shoes on the stairs soon quieted. Joel looked at Megan, thinking of the happiness she brought Lacy, of the feelings she stirred within him. Feelings he fought because Megan planned to leave Paradise.

But for all Megan talked of leaving to build a career in photography, he couldn't help thinking it was something she could do right here in Paradise. Claire had mentioned a picture she'd taken of her granddaughter. Maybe she could open her own studio.

Megan pushed back her hair. He knew he was staring at her, but he couldn't seem to help it. His mind kept forming pictures of its own; of Megan and Lacy sharing more secrets, some of the three of them together, one of just him and Megan. His gaze dropped to her mouth, to lips that had felt soft and willing beneath his. He wanted to kiss her again....

"Joel! Megan!" Lacy was calling from downstairs, her voice that of a hungry, tired child.

"I didn't mean to stay so long."

Megan's words were tremulous and Joel gave a sigh over his daughter's timing. He encompassed the room with one last look, feeling a fresh amazement over the transformation Megan had brought about. "I didn't mean for you to do all this. Thanks."

She smiled then, leaving him filled with wanting as he followed her down the stairs. Lacy was waiting for them on the porch, hugging Ted, wanting Megan to stay for supper.

"Molly's waiting for me to come home and feed her," Megan said, giving Lacy's braid a playful tug.

"You're welcome to stay." Joel watched Megan's gaze trail lingeringly up his chest, then stop at his mouth.

Almost wistfully she told him, "I'd better go."

Her words caused Lacy to pout, but Megan simply caught his daughter's hand and walked to her truck, making plans for Lacy's next visit with her. When Megan climbed in the cab, Lacy raced back to his side. As they watched her drive away, Joel wondered how things might change if Megan were to stay in Paradise.

Megan tucked in her shirt and fluffed her hair around her shoulders, then stood back from the mirror for a critical look. The ivory shirt with its western yoke and matching skirt were beautiful, a gift her father had brought her from Arizona. But she couldn't help thinking Suzanne could have given the outfit a little more flair. Megan flipped up the collar of the shirt, then shook her head in frustration. She looked *silly,* not sophisticated, the way she wanted to look tonight.

There was a soft knock at the bedroom door, then Suzanne peeked in. "Megan, come on. Dad's waiting."

Megan shoved her hands through her hair, the ten minutes she'd spent brushing it forgotten. Maybe if she wore some jewelry... Rummaging through the small box on her dresser, she told Suzanne over her shoulder, "Tell him I'll be right there."

The door clicked shut. Unable to find the small gold clips she sought, Megan scattered jewelry on the dresser top, catching her lip as she searched through the tangle of beads and chains and earrings she'd collected at birthdays and Christmases over the years.

"Need some help?"

Megan jumped, her hand at her heart. "Suzanne! I thought you'd gone downstairs."

Suzanne caught her sister's hands before Megan could drag them through her hair again. "Let me fix your collar."

Megan stood obediently, used to this role reversal. In everything else, she'd taken care of her sister. But when it came to fashion, Suzanne was the expert. Megan sighed, eyeing her sister's trendy, clinging outfit and matching high-heeled shoes.

"I can't help but wonder who you're going to all this trouble for," Suzanne teased, giving Megan a staying gesture before she turned to pick through the jewelry. She came up with a pair of small silver and turquoise earrings, which she expertly fastened while Megan fidgeted.

"This is an important dinner for Dad," Megan said in defense of her uncharacteristic fussing. But she found herself thinking of Joel, of the way he'd looked the other day from her view out Lacy's bedroom window. He'd stood before the fence he was mending, staring across a grassy pasture. The sun's rays had seemed to bounce off his tawny hair, a light breeze gathering to lift the strands from his forehead. Then he'd pulled at the snaps on his shirt, tugged it open to bare his chest and shrugged it from his golden shoulders, all the while taking her breath away. He'd tossed it carelessly on the ground while she'd watched in rapture until Lacy called her name. Her mouth felt dry, remembering.

Megan gave her head a shake and forced a smile for Suzanne. "I'm just trying to be like you, for a change."

"Don't, Meg. Don't try to be someone you're not." Suzanne had sobered, her hand pressed to her stomach in a gesture Megan had seen her repeat throughout the hour since she'd arrived. A gesture that elicited concern.

Megan caught her sister's shoulders, no longer concerned about clothes. "What is it, Suzanne? Is your stomach hurting you?"

Suzanne shook her head in dismissal, pulling away, the pain seeming to pass. "I'm fine now."

"You're not fine at all. Tell me what's wrong."

Suzanne mustered a smile, though it was obvious the pain lingered. "You were always such a mother hen."

"Suzanne..."

"All right. Dad meant for me to tell you while I was here, anyway. I'm surprised he hasn't already, the way he's been fussing—"

"Suzanne, please."

"There's nothing to be worried about, Meg. I have an ulcer. That's all."

Megan stared at her sister in disbelief. An ulcer. "That's impossible. Ulcers are something stressed-out adults get, not teenagers."

"That's what I thought, too."

But the pain in her sister's eyes left no room for doubt for either of them.

"Don't look so stricken, Meg. I'm just a little tense about starting college. I've got medication and the doctor says I should be better in no time. Come on now. Let's go. Dad said he was starving. Something to eat will help settle my stomach and *your* nerves." Suzanne turned away, then stopped. Megan followed her sister's gaze to the doll lying on the bed.

She'd forgotten to put Suzanne's doll away after Lacy had played with it the other day. Megan noticed for the first time that the doll's hair was mussed, the velvet dress rumpled. Aware the doll had been special to Suzanne, Megan said contritely, "I'm sorry about the doll. I let Lacy play with it one day. She was very careful, but I shouldn't have—"

"No. It's okay. Really. Let her play with it anytime." Leaving the doll where it lay, Suzanne left the room.

Megan looked after her sister in surprise, remembering how upset Suzanne would get if Megan so much as moved the doll on its shelf. Had Suzanne outgrown that particular obsession?

Downstairs, Megan found her father waiting, tugging at his tie. She stopped and stared, struck by how handsome he still was. The touch of silver in his dark hair was striking, the almond eyes he'd handed down to his daughters, compelling. He'd never seemed to lead much of a social life that she could recall, only occasionally leaving her and Suzanne in the care of the Taylors so he could spend a night out. Looking at him now, she was certain he had never lacked for opportunity. But even when she and Suzanne were older, he'd seldom dated. She could suddenly appreciate the extent to which he'd put his daughters first.

"You look great, Dad." Megan went to her father, giving him an impulsive hug. Maybe once Suzanne was in college and she was off to California, her father would find someone special to share his life with. Her thoughts turned to Patrice, an ache welling within her. She would never really understand what had driven her mother away.

And she wondered, even if she found Patrice, would she ever understand why her mother had deserted her and Suzanne?

They left the house and Megan pushed the troubling thought aside, trying to enjoy herself at the famed Circle R, while keeping a concerned watch over her sister. The restaurant was just as she remembered from her last visit. Candles burning in red globes, slow dreamy music. Megan touched the pearl buttons on her shirt, admiring the wagon-wheel chandelier that flickered overhead. She felt comfortable in these surroundings. The feeling of anticipation curling inside her was somehow right, too. Megan looked toward the entrance, watching for Joel and Lacy, certain the little girl would want to sit beside her. In her purse, she'd brought a copy of her favorite photo of Lacy and Molly to give to Joel.

She was thinking of Joel, expecting him, yet her breath caught when he filled the doorway. There was no hat to hide his blue-gray eyes as his gaze swept the room.

Megan drank in the sight of him. His hair was brushed neatly back, curving thickly over the collar of a western-cut jacket that matched its wheat color. His shirt was a stark white contrast to his tanned skin. In a light-striped tie, he was devastating, but Megan had to grin at the pressed blue jeans he'd worn over a pair of fine leather boots.

He stepped into the reception area, and Megan was surprised to see he was alone. Even as she missed Lacy's presence, Megan felt her heart speed into an erratic beat. Joel was now looking at her, only her, and she felt like a girl again, about to go on a first date with the man of her dreams. . . .

"Joel!" Her father had risen and was waving Joel over. The restaurant was busy and as Joel crossed the room, Megan became aware of the heads of the ladies turning.

"Now I know why you fussed so much getting ready," Suzanne teased in her ear. But Megan was too busy struggling for composure to reply.

As the men took their seats, Matt asked after Lacy.

"Lacy's staying the night with Claire Evanston and her granddaughter, Jennifer," Joel explained, his gaze skimming to Megan, touching her face, her hair, and drifting over the ivory outfit. A warmth spread through Megan at the glow in his eyes, and she wondered if he had purposely made arrangements for Lacy to be elsewhere, wanting to spend this time with her.

Matt went on to reacquaint Joel and Suzanne. Watching Suzanne flash a smile at him, Megan wished once again that she had some of her sister's style and poise. But the feeling faded with the realization that Joel wasn't looking at Suzanne the same way he'd looked at her, that she seemed to please him just as she was.

As her father had promised, talk of the store was kept to a minimum, the men agreeing to meet there in the morning, then move on to the realtor's office. Matt was more interested in tales of the rodeo and Joel seemed willing to oblige. Megan was drawn to listen, trying to fit Lacy and the rodeo queen, Luann, into the exciting pictures he drew with his words.

"You must miss the competition," Matt observed.

Joel shrugged. "I still rodeo some, but I want to cut down."

"What about the prestige?" Suzanne asked, obviously impressed with Joel's record. "Megan said you were All-Round Champion once. That had to give you a bit of a thrill."

"Yeah, it did. But that takes a lot of campaigning. A lot of hard work. I'm getting too old for that." Joel chuckled, then his laughter died. "I guess somewhere along the way, the prestige lost its appeal. Different things matter to me now."

Megan stilled as Joel's gaze settled upon her.

"We all change as we grow." Matt sighed, watching Joel watch his daughter, the look in the younger man's eyes convincing him Megan was one of those things that mattered. He wondered if he'd ever looked at Patrice quite that way. Maybe if he had, Patrice wouldn't have tired of waiting for him to keep all those promises of a better life. Now it looked as if this boy was going to suffer for his mistakes. He knew the real reason Megan was leaving Paradise. Knew she wouldn't stay, despite the look in Joel Crawford's eyes. Guilt closed around his heart. Years ago, he thought he'd made the best decision for his daughters. But he shouldn't have lied to them.

"I'd have to agree these girls of yours have changed," Joel finally said, smoothing over the lengthening silence. "They don't have bruises all over their knees from falling off their bikes."

When he smiled at her, Megan blushed, his words bringing to mind the day she'd bandaged Lacy's knee; how Lacy had gone outside and the kiss that had followed. Joel had wanted to kiss her again that same evening and she wondered if he still did, if he planned to tonight.

All of a sudden, her sister half rose, gasping in pain.

Clutching her stomach, Suzanne braced a hand against the table and sent it rocking.

"Suzanne!" Megan jumped up, fear flashing through her. She reached for Suzanne, but her father was already at her sister's side, with Joel on his heels.

"Easy, Suzanne." Matt steadied his daughter until she could sink back into her chair. The hostess appeared, but after exchanging a quick look with Suzanne, Matt held the woman at bay with a shake of his head.

Megan knelt beside Suzanne, oblivious to the curious stares of the customers. "Suzanne, are you okay?"

To her relief, Suzanne's discomfort seemed to subside. "Don't worry, Megan. I think that meal I just ate didn't agree with my ulcer, that's all. I'm feeling better already."

"I think we'll call it a night all the same." Matt patted Suzanne's shoulder and turned to Joel. "Will you see Megan home?"

"Of course."

"I'm going with you," Megan said quickly, not quite over the scare her sister had given her.

"I'm *fine,*" Suzanne insisted, and Megan felt her father's warning hand on her shoulder. Reluctantly, she rose.

"There's dessert and coffee on the way." Matt slipped a bill on the table. "You two stay and enjoy it."

"I'm just tired now," Suzanne assured them, and Megan had to admit that much seemed true. Her sister was pale, eyes rimmed with fatigue.

Matt helped Suzanne rise and they started toward the door.

Megan hesitated, then realizing she hadn't been very polite, almost leaving Joel stranded, she took her seat. Together they watched Matt and Suzanne leave, Megan with a knot in her throat.

"I'm not much on dessert," Joel said pointedly. "How about we give them a head start, then go check on Suzanne?"

He didn't need to ask twice. Minutes later, they crossed the parking lot to Joel's pickup and climbed inside. He wasted no time heading them down the road, reassuring her as he did. "There are a lot of good medicines to treat ulcers now. I don't mean to make light of it, but Suzanne probably will be fine."

Megan shot him a grateful glance, then said curiously, "You sound as if you're speaking from experience."

"My dad had an ulcer when I was in my teens. He used to kid me, say I gave him that ulcer and gray hair, too. The true cause was supposed to be the bad times that had fallen on small farmers. Things were pretty tight for a while back then, but Dad managed to hang on to the farm."

Megan nodded in understanding, having learned that leaner times had often been at the bottom of her parents' arguments.

"But now that I'm raising a child of my own," Joel continued with a grin, "I think maybe he wasn't kidding, after all."

Megan laughed then. The knot in her throat had disappeared and she knew she had Joel to thank. They rode in silence, a warm kind of quiet that made her feel as if Joel held her hand securely in his. She had thought it would take forever to get home, but before she knew it, they were pulling into the driveway.

One light burned dimly in the front-room window, the same light she'd left glowing that first night she'd waited for Joel to come home. Noting the upstairs lights were out, Megan murmured in relief, "Suzanne must have gone right to bed."

The truck rolled to a stop and Joel shifted into Park, letting the truck idle. "Did your dad used to wait up for you?"

In the process of trying to form a goodbye in her mind and reach reluctantly for the door handle, Megan looked over in surprise at Joel's teasing tone. He'd loosened his tie as he drove, completely unknotting the silk and letting it hang. With one arm slung over the steering wheel and a mischievous grin on his face, he looked all of eighteen again. A laugh escaped before Megan could stop it.

"Yes," she admitted. "Though more often for Suzanne. There was never a chance for either of us to steal a kiss in the driveway. Dad would always be right there to turn on the porch light as soon as our dates pulled in."

"I'd have gotten my kiss," Joel said with typical male confidence.

And though Megan didn't doubt that he would have, she challenged, "How would you have managed that?"

"I'd have stopped in the lane down the road." Joel's eyes twinkled as he gave a nod toward the house. "No porch light. Ten to one, he's asleep on the couch. Ten years ago, I'd have taken my chances and kissed you again, right here.''

Kissed you... Megan tried to reply, but her throat was all tight again, the sound of her heartbeat filling her ears while her blood rushed hotly through her veins. Joel turned to face her, his arm creeping across the back of the seat.

''This outfit you're wearing, it's real pretty. Soft.'' His fingers toyed with the material of her collar, his eyes lighting with appreciation, making her feel like that doll in the box again. Then he touched the silver and turquoise at her ear and she shivered.

''You make me feel like taking chances again, Megan,'' he whispered, his tone no longer teasing.

He filled his hand with her hair, pulling her closer. He smelled good, like a mix of warm summer breeze and cool summer night. Megan felt herself melting into his arms, enticed by the scent of him, the feel of him, the look in his eyes. They were dark with desire, and something more.

Megan faltered, aware for the first time that Lacy was not the only one she could hurt if she wasn't careful. But the need in Joel's eyes was almost more than she could turn away from.

''Megan?''

As his whisper passed warmly over her skin, she shivered, the chill sweeping the length of her.

''What's wrong?''

His hand tightened in her hair, then loosened, and Megan slipped from his arms, pushing strands from her face with a trembling hand. It was so hard to do the right thing. But she couldn't give in to these feelings she had for Joel when she didn't know where her search for Patrice might lead or how long it might take. "I'm sorry. This just isn't right, not when I'll be leaving."

Long seconds of silence passed. Then Joel said quietly, "It doesn't have to be like this."

Megan slipped Lacy's picture from her purse. She wished she could explain to Joel the need she had to find her mother. But he wouldn't understand any more than he understood Lacy's feelings for Luann.

"I'm sorry," she repeated, forcing a firmness into her voice. She pushed the picture into his hands and reached for the door handle.

"Megan, wait—"

But she didn't wait, afraid she might end up hurting them all. She hurried to the house and went inside, closing the door and listening to the sound of Joel's pickup churning up gravel, then gradually fading.

You've done the right thing. You've done the right thing.

Her father stirred on the couch then and Megan tiptoed into the living room. He'd obviously just awakened, and was tossing off the afghan he'd pulled over himself. Remembering Joel's teasing, Megan gave a painful smile.

Matt glanced at the clock on the wall, then patted the couch seat beside him. "You're home early."

Megan sank onto the soft cushions. "How's Suzanne?"

"She was asleep ten minutes after we walked through the door. Guess I was, too," Matt said, chuckling. Then he sobered, seeing the worry on his daughter's face. "She's going to be fine, Megan."

"I know. I just hate to see her hurting."

Matt patted her hand, glad she'd missed the worst of Suzanne's pain before the medication was started. His gaze searched her face. Megan was hurting, too, in her own way. With each day that passed, he grew more certain that he'd made a mistake. That his daughters would have to know the truth.

"Why don't we go check on her, Dad?" Her father looked tired. And there was something troubling in the way his worried gaze seemed to fall upon her as often as drift up the stairs to where Suzanne slept. He said nothing, though, and she followed him up to Suzanne's bedroom, finding some reassurance in the sight of her sister sleeping peacefully.

With a good-night kiss for her father, Megan went to her room. It was dark and quiet and Megan left it that way, going to the window. She pulled up a chair and nudged off her shoes, sitting down and spreading her skirt over her knees, her fingers unconsciously smoothing the fabric Joel had admired.

Her gaze lifted to the stars and she wondered as she had every night since she was ten, where Patrice might be. Was her mother thinking of her now? Maybe living in regret for having left her and Suzanne? Or would Megan's leaving here be in vain, giving her no answers—or at least none that she wanted to hear.

Megan sighed. Her quest to find her mother was no longer something she wanted to do, only something she *had* to do. She knew the reason why as she watched the lights at the Crawford farm flicker on in the distance.

Joel rocked back in the kitchen chair, nursing a beer, cooling down. He'd been frustrated, angry. But he wasn't about to give up on Megan. He had all night to sit and think of a plan, a way to convince her to stay.

Taking a long pull on his beer, he set down the can. He lifted the picture Megan had given him, feeling badly for having tossed it on the table along with his hat. He'd been in no frame of mind to look at it before, but he was curious now and held it out of the glare of the overhead light.

What he saw hit hard.

Lacy's hair had an almost ethereal glow; the old mare eating apples from the little girl's hand was textured with age. Any other time, the delight on his daughter's face would have made him smile. Now it made him realize it wasn't the color, the pose, the technicalities of the print that drew and held him. It was the emotion. A poignant story of the passage of time caught in one brief instant.

He understood then, the reality of Megan's leaving. Her talent was something God-given, something she couldn't ignore. He knew because he understood. His hand with a horse and dexterity with a rope were God-given, too. Megan's desire to create a picture was as strong—probably stronger—than his will to compete had ever been. Megan wouldn't be whole without reaching the goal she'd set for herself. She would never be satisfied, stuck here in Paradise, when a world of pictures were waiting to be taken.

An ache welled within him. He wished he didn't have all night to sit and think.

Chapter Seven

The next evening, Megan was waiting on the porch swing when Joel arrived with Lacy, just as they had planned at the tack shop that morning. Since Joel would be leaving for Kearny at daybreak, they'd thought it best that Lacy spend the night.

Watching Joel climb from the truck, Megan tucked her hands in the wide pockets of her lavender dress. Her hair... Still damp from her shower, it hung loosely around her shoulders. She should have done something with it.

"We can have a treat, Megan!" Lacy ran over, carrying a bag of cookies and smelling like baby shampoo. Apparently, Lacy had already had supper and a bath. Megan's heart sank a little and she pushed aside the idea of the three of them sharing supper before Joel left.

Rising, she waited for him to cross the yard and set Lacy's small suitcase on the porch, feeling drawn by his every move. Joel appeared to have showered, too, his hair dampening the collar of his sky-blue shirt. His freshly shaven skin had taken some sun today and Megan wondered if he'd been working on the fence again, with his chest bare to the burning rays.

"Did Matt and Suzanne get off okay?"

Megan let out a breath, suddenly realizing Lacy had run off to swing. "They left after lunch. Dad's pretty busy getting the new store started."

"I'm coming to know that feeling," Joel said, maintaining a polite distance. But his expression had brightened and she knew he was pleased he owned the store now. It made her feel good, knowing the shop her father had worked so hard to establish would be in good hands. After years of waiting to leave, she felt a sadness, an emptiness, at the thought that she would be putting all that behind her.

Joel glanced away, and the empty feeling inside her intensified until she knew she was only fooling herself. Leaving Joel and Lacy behind was what really troubled her.

Lacy returned then, hugging Megan's leg, and she ruffled the little girl's hair, wanting nothing more than to scoop Lacy up in her arms.

"Look," Joel said suddenly, "don't worry about opening the shop tomorrow afternoon. I know you've got a lot on your mind with the sale of the store. Having to watch Lacy—"

"Lacy's no trouble. Really. Besides, you get a lot of business on Sunday afternoons." Megan managed a smile that faded when he didn't return it.

"I want to work," Lacy added. "I want to sweep and try on the jewelry."

Joel gave in then, the faint curve of his lips directed at his daughter. "I'll leave it up to Megan, then." Satisfied, Lacy plunked down on the step with her cookies. Joel cast Megan a glance and said quietly, "Whatever you decide is fine. You're still running the store. Nothing's changed."

But it had, and they both knew it. He'd come to terms with the fact that she would be leaving. Watching Joel hug Lacy goodbye, she understood that, like her father, he meant to put his daughter first. She had to do the same.

But in leaving Paradise, was she? As she and Lacy stood hand in hand to see Joel off, it didn't seem so.

As good as his word, Joel spent the first half of August hitting one rodeo after another all across the state. Megan couldn't help noticing that, although Lacy loved coming to stay the night, each time he left, she watched after him a little longer. She talked of the rodeo, of riding Tally and cheering for Joel. It wasn't hard to see that Lacy was missing her dad and the good times they had at the rodeo.

But Lacy, it seemed, had the perfect solution. As Joel's pickup and trailer disappeared down the road one evening, headed for the Gordon rodeo, Lacy announced, "I want us to go with next time, Megan."

"That's a nice idea, Lacy, but I need to watch over the store and I don't think your dad—"

"He said you can come."

"Oh." Surprise had her holding her tongue. She and Joel had been very careful to keep things impersonal between them. This was the last thing she had expected. "That was nice of him, Lacy, but I really don't think I should."

"But my dad misses me," Lacy said, and the child's sadness wound its way around Megan's heart.

"Oh, sweetheart." Megan knelt and took Lacy's small hands in hers. "Anytime you want, your dad will take you to the rodeo with him. He only leaves you here because he thinks it makes you happy."

"But I want to be with you, too." Sudden tears spilled over Lacy's cheeks and she pulled her hands free, flinging her arms around Megan's neck.

Guilt shot through Megan like a spear. No matter what she did, it would be wrong. She stood, taking Lacy up with her, holding the little girl tight, feeling the child's love and unable to keep from returning it. "It's all right, Lacy. It's all right."

Lacy raised a tear-stained face from Megan's shoulder. "Will you go to the rodeo with me and Joel?"

"Yes. I'll go to the very next rodeo."

"Promise?"

"I promise." Megan crossed her heart, and wished she could promise more.

Chapter Eight

After four hours on the road, Joel turned his rig into Megan's driveway, the Gordon rodeo and the setting sun behind him. As soon as the roping was over, he'd pulled out, wanting to get back at a decent hour to take Lacy home. It had been a long trip, and the sight of his daughter and Megan sitting on the porch step eating ice-cream cones gave him his first smile of the day.

But lately, that warm feeling of homecoming wasn't enough to carry him through the next rodeo. When Lacy had asked if Megan could come to a rodeo, he'd agreed, for the idea of having them with him held more appeal.

Joel opened the truck door and slid out, gratefully stretching his legs to the ground. Even with the sky turning a shadowy purple at his back, the sun's record-breaking heat still clung to the countryside. Joel brushed the last layer of arena dust from his black shirt and walked toward the porch. His timing had been off that afternoon, but it looked as if it was right on the money now as Lacy came running over, giving him a hug and offering a bite of ice cream. The cold taste of vanilla was refreshing and sweet, and so was the sight of Megan, trying to catch the melting drops on the side of her cone. She was wearing her little green shirt with her jeans, her cheeks flushed pink from the heat and her hair pulled into a braid like Lacy's. As he walked, his gaze lingered on her dainty, curling tongue until Lacy demanded his attention.

"Joel! Megan's going with us to the very next rodeo!"

"Is that so?" Trying to hide the leap of his heart, Joel handed Lacy her cone and settled the little girl back on the step. He glanced at Megan. Judging by the worry in her eyes, her decision to come to a rodeo hadn't been made lightly.

She patted Lacy's knee. "Why don't you go find Ted and get those ham sandwiches out of the refrigerator?"

Lacy beamed up at Joel. "I made them for you."

"She really did," Megan said, and Joel watched her fond gaze follow Lacy into the house. Then she looked up at him, her eyes reflecting the deep concern he'd known since the day his daughter was born. "Lacy cried after you left today. She was pretty upset. I'm afraid she's not happy here—"

"Don't even think that." Megan cared for his daughter in a way Luann never had. "Lacy wants to be here with you."

"Yes, but she misses you after you've gone."

Joel sighed, and sank onto the step next to Megan. In trying to do what was best for Lacy, he and Megan had only succeeded in making her have to choose between them.

Lacy came out the door then, with Ted under her arm and a bag of sandwiches in her hand. Joel's gaze jumped to Lacy, then back to Megan in frustration. If only...

Joel cut the thought short. He had no right to wish away Megan's dreams. But with each day that passed, he was more dissatisfied with the way things were, with the way things soon would be.

For now, the best he could do was to put Megan's mind at ease. He pushed back his hat and gave Lacy's braid a tug. "How do you feel about spending your birthday with Megan at the Atkinson rodeo?"

Lacy bounced on the porch step, all but losing the sandwiches and Ted. "I want to!"

"They have a fair with rides and games. And plenty of good food." Joel gave Megan a grin. "Atkinson's only a half hour away. I used to rodeo there in my younger days."

"Then I guess you know what you're doing."

Megan sounded uncertain and Joel quietly assured her, "It will be okay."

"It will be *fun*," Lacy chimed in. "They always have pony rides at fairs."

To Joel's relief, Megan laughed. "Then I wouldn't want to miss it."

"Bring your camera," Joel suggested.

"I'll do that." Her eyes shone, and he knew she was already taking pictures in her mind, capturing the spirit of a small-town fair and rodeo. Hope burned to life within him that the day spent together would bring her to see the same picture that kept forming in his mind.

In keeping with his optimistic mood, the day of the fair was sunny, with a cool front bringing pleasant relief from the heat. Lacy prodded him to hurry through every step of the morning from breakfast to loading Tally, until they finally pulled into Megan's driveway. Megan came out the front door, her hair hanging loose, wearing a bright pink shirt, frosted jeans and new cream-colored boots that reminded him of the way she'd been dressed that first day he'd stopped at the store. Joel grinned down at Lacy. His daughter had worn the same, with the addition of her pink straw hat.

Megan climbed in the truck, handing Lacy a rainbow-striped package with a matching bow. "Happy birthday, Lacy."

"Ohh..." Lacy savored the pretty wrapping for just five seconds, then pulled at the ribbons, making Megan laugh while Joel admonished her to slow down. When Lacy pulled out her new camera with its neon pink casing, he didn't have to remind her about thank-yous. She threw her arms around Megan's neck and cried, "My very own! Thank you! Thank you!"

Megan hugged Lacy back, her hesitant gaze meeting Joel's over his daughter's shoulder. As if she felt a need to explain her gift giving, she murmured, "Lacy's really quite good with a camera."

He didn't doubt it. He remembered the evening he'd gotten back early from the nearby Chambers rodeo. As he'd walked up to Megan's porch, Lacy had snapped his picture with an expensive-looking camera, sounding like a professional when she told him to say cheese.

"I'm going to take a picture of you when you win today, Joel," Lacy announced while she peered at him through the lens.

With a laugh, he gave her hat a tug. "Guess I'd better win, then. Wouldn't want to disappoint the birthday girl."

"Sounds like the pressure's on," Megan said, one corner of her mouth lifting.

"I usually come through when there's a couple of pretty faces in the stands to cheer me on," Joel teased, unable to hide his pleasure at having Megan with him. Satisfied with the flare of color he'd brought to her cheeks, he dragged his gaze to the road and pointed the rig north to Atkinson.

Listening to Lacy describe to Megan the birthday doll and pink jeans he'd given her, Joel sobered, staring through the windshield down the straight stretch of highway. It had been a difficult decision to make, but this year, there had been no "gift" from Luann to Lacy. He'd called Lacy's mother. Now all he could do was be there for his little girl.

Determined to make Lacy's birthday a happy one, Joel pushed his worries from his mind. He realized how much he'd missed Lacy's chatter on the lone road trips he'd been making. And Megan seemed to naturally fill a space that had been empty for too long. In no time at all, they'd reached their destination.

Set on flat-lying plain with the sun blazing overhead, Atkinson hadn't changed much. Joel parked his rig among the rest, exchanging howdys with familiar faces, introducing Megan to some of the cowboys' wives and sweethearts. They went about the tasks of unloading and getting his number for the roping event, stopping for a quick bite to eat before returning to get Tally saddled.

Megan wanted pictures of him and Lacy in the rodeo's Grand Entry and Joel obliged, lifting Lacy to ride behind him. They followed the parade of competitors in a lope around the arena, finally lining up in the center. For Joel, the sun was somehow brighter, just knowing Megan was here to share the moment with him and Lacy.

When Joel turned Tally toward the gate, Megan was there waiting, talking with some of the women she'd met and looking like a seasoned cowgirl. He was struck by the way she fit so easily into his life. And he wondered how different things might have been if Megan had been standing at that gate ten years ago, before he'd ever met Luann.

But then, he wouldn't have Lacy.

With that thought, Joel felt the weight of the past lifting, the sense of failure he'd carried so long, fading. He was ready now, to start a new life for Lacy—and for himself. Feeling his daughter's small arms tighten around him, he nudged Tally into a trot and rode over to Megan. She raised her camera and he grinned for her.

"I need to ride Tally around and loosen him up a little more," he told Megan.

"I have to help," Lacy added.

Joel chuckled, explaining, "Once on board, Lacy usually has to be pried off Tally's back."

Megan waved them on with a grin. "I came to watch you win, cowboy. I'm not going to stand in the way."

She stayed busy with her camera while Joel rode out back of the chutes, eventually relinquishing his place in the saddle to Lacy and leading Tally around. When the saddle-bronc riding ended, the roping began. Megan coaxed Lacy out of the saddle with the pink camera and they walked up near the arena.

Joel's mouth curved wryly, watching the cowboys perk up at the sight of Megan, trying to impress her as they stretched and flexed their muscles to warm up for their events. Then he was called on deck and Joel mounted, readying his rope, anticipation tingling down his spine. For so long, this had been no more than a job to him. Now he found himself wanting to make an impression.

"Good luck." Holding Lacy's hand, Megan marveled at the transformation that stole over Joel. He'd shoved down his hat, his lips firming, his eyes darkening with intent, while the horse, who had been standing quietly, came to life beneath him. He caught her by surprise with his sudden grin, then rode off, entering the arena to a swell of applause when the announcer called his name.

Megan stared after him, pride welling up within her, making her heart pound and her breath catch—and Joel wasn't even competing yet. He looked magnificent in his crisp white shirt and dove-gray hat and boots, but seeing him here at the rodeo, she knew he was more than a handsome face in the crowd. He was a professional, well-liked and respected by his peers.

Megan looked down at Lacy, thinking Joel was also a much-loved father. She could no longer recall where the notion had come from that he was lacking as a parent. What he and Lacy shared was special. Being here with them, she felt a part of that specialness, too.

Joel backed Tally into the box and Lacy let go of Megan's hand to take pictures. Megan laced her fingers tightly, her camera forgotten, her breath stalled in her lungs as she watched, entranced by the quivering horse held in check by the steady sureness of Joel's hand. With a nod, he signaled the release of the calf.

Megan's heart jumped when Tally bounded out of the box. Joel's wrist flicked and the loop sang out and dropped with precision over the head of the calf. He was out of the saddle before Tally slid to a stop and down the length of rope when the calf hit the end. Tally backed against the sudden weight and kept the rope taut while the calf was thrown, the horse no longer resembling the gentle mount that had carried Lacy around. Piggin string in hand, Joel made his tie and threw his hands high, his time recorded by the officials.

Joel mounted and rode Tally forward. The tension on the rope eased. The tie held. The announcer boomed out what was to be the winning time of nine and four-tenths seconds, drawing a cheer from the crowd and whoops from Lacy and Megan.

After tending to Tally, Joel led the way to the grandstand. Megan enjoyed watching the rest of the rodeo while sitting among some of the cowboys and their families. Word of Lacy's birthday soon spread, and the cowboys endeared themselves to Megan as they spoiled the "little cowgirl" with candy and quarters. When the rodeo was over, Joel checked on Tally, then declared it was time to hit the midway.

Joel impressed Megan with his skill at the games, winning Lacy her choice of stuffed animals until the carnies waved him away. Daylight faded and the carnival came to life in a rainbow of whirling lights. Depositing Lacy's neon critters in the pickup, they headed for the rides.

They'd stopped for corn dogs, curly fries and fresh lemonade, when Megan heard a familiar voice call their names. She turned to see Claire walking toward them, with red-haired Jennifer skipping along.

"Looks like all of Paradise came to see Joel Crawford rope," Claire teased.

"We came here for my birthday," Lacy corrected her. "I'm five years old today."

"Well then, we want to help celebrate, don't we, Jennifer?" The little girl at Claire's side grinned and grasped Lacy's hand. "How about letting me steal Lacy for an hour, Joel?"

"Can I go with them, please?" Lacy pleaded.

Joel questioned Megan with a quick glance that gave the moment a feeling of intimacy, like that of the husband checking with the wife. Megan was unaware that she'd smiled until she heard Joel say, "It's okay with us. Just make sure you girls behave."

The little girls sang out a chorus of promises to be good. While she chatted with Claire, Megan observed Joel give a low lecture to Lacy and Jennifer and slip them each some money. He agreed to meet Claire near the entrance in an hour, explaining they would be there with the rig. Claire was soon headed down the midway, with Jennifer and Lacy taking turns looking through the pink camera still slung around Lacy's neck.

Megan felt Joel's hand at the small of her back and looked into his eyes, and the night seemed to suddenly take on a new atmosphere. She stared at his handsome face, her palms growing damp and her cheeks burning as she tried to guess what he was thinking, what they would do next. The cozy feeling had vanished, replaced by the excitement and uncertainty of a first date—except that Joel's gaze hinted at a greater intimacy, making her heart beat fast and hard.

Joel bought her cotton candy and started them slowly back to the truck and trailer, laying claim to her hand somewhere along the way. The lights and the noise gradually dimmed behind them, giving way to a starlit quiet that enhanced the warm feeling that coursed from his hand to hers. Megan fought to keep her perspective, to think of Lacy and of Patrice and California. With Lacy to consider, she was certain Joel would do the same. But she couldn't help dreaming of what might have been, the way she had as a girl.

They reached the rig and Joel let go of her hand. Megan sighed wistfully, only to find she'd used her last breath as he turned her into his arms and kissed her.

Joel's mouth fastened over hers with a sureness that stunned her, that left no room for misgivings. Dropping her candy from limp fingers, Megan wound her arms around Joel's neck, pouring all the emotion she'd stored up that day into the embrace. Safe in the cocoon made by the horse and trailer, she pressed against him, letting him take the kiss deeper, his mouth staying sealed over hers until they both gasped for air.

She made a sound that was part moan, part laugh, part sigh. Looking up, Megan savored the perfection of his features, basking in the feel of his gaze upon her, caught up in a dream come true. Megan's eyes drifted closed as Joel's hand glided upward, his palm finding her breast.

"This feeling is special." Joel's voice was husky, his hand hot. His thumb traced her nipple through the soft cotton of her shirt and her eyes fluttered open, her gaze meeting the haze of desire in his. Then he kissed her quickly, his hand lowering to take hold of hers, his next words insistent. "But there's more. You feel it, too, Megan. I—"

"Joel!"

The call of his name intruded, jolting them, the frantic sound of Claire's voice sending Megan's thoughts whirling to Lacy. Joel spun around, keeping hold of her hand.

Claire rushed up to them, Jennifer running at her side. Without prelude, she gasped, "I can't find Lacy!"

Chapter Nine

Can't find Lacy.

This feeling is special. But there's more...

Can't find Lacy.

The phrases warred in Megan's mind for attention. But as she watched Joel pale beneath his tan, felt his fingers tighten around her hand, the reality of Claire's words chilled her.

Claire pulled her granddaughter close to her side. "Jennifer was taking a turn at a game and Lacy and I were watching. I looked down a moment later and Lacy was gone."

Megan glanced through the darkness in the direction of the midway, the noise of the crowd drifting down. The thought of Lacy alone among all those strangers had every frightening story on childnapping she'd ever heard filling her head, sending a wave of pure dread washing over her.

"Where did you last see her?" Joel asked Claire.

"By the dart game. Jennifer was throwing darts at balloons. I waited there, thinking Lacy had to be close by, but when she didn't come back, I came to find you."

"Why don't you take Jennifer there now and watch for Lacy. Megan and I will search the midway." Joel gave the distraught Claire a reassuring look. "Lacy's an old hand at these fairs. We'll find her."

Not wasting another moment, they began their search, leaving Claire and Jennifer near the dart game. Megan tried to find comfort in Joel's words. But Lacy wasn't an old hand at anything. She was a child, small and helpless and alone.

"I'll take this side of the midway," Joel said. "You head down the other."

Megan hated to let go of his hand. She looked down the midway at the lights and the crowd, feeling an inch away from panic.

"Megan?"

Megan glanced up to find Joel looking at her with concern, despite the turmoil he had to be feeling. Knowing they would run less chance of missing Lacy if they split up, Megan released his hand. "Let's go."

Joel cupped her cheek with his hand, then he was gone.

Now the bright colors and musical sounds of the fair seemed garish and intrusive to Megan. She forced herself to go slow, fearful of passing by Lacy in the ebb and flow of the crowd. Her heart wavered in its beat each time she spotted a blond ponytail.

Megan paused a moment near the haunted house, shivering as she stared at the eerie mansion. Frowning, she glanced away, unable to imagine Lacy chancing the ghosts alone. The games had been a big hit, and also the cotton candy booth, and Lacy had loved the pony rides. . . .

That was it. Megan pushed through the crowd gathered by the dunk tank, making her way to the far end of the midway where ten fat ponies plodded around a well-worn path. Watching them from the arms of a short, bandy-legged cowboy she had met earlier, was Lacy.

Thank God . . . Megan closed her eyes on the brief, heartfelt prayer. She ran past the taco stand that served as the last divider of the midway and turned to look up the other side, spotting Joel farther back. She called his name. Catching his gaze over the crowd, she pointed wordlessly to Lacy.

Joel's big shoulders slumped, and Megan swore she saw his knees go weak. She knew hers trembled. He shouldered his way through the milling people, stopping at her side, his eyes dark with gratitude.

"Joel!" Lacy had seen them, and the sound of her happy voice brought a look of both relief and exasperation to Joel's face. He strode over to the cowboy who transferred Lacy into his arms.

"Thanks, Mac." The husky timbre of Joel's voice caused a tightening in Megan's chest.

"Heck, I knew you'd be along soon to find this little gal." Red-faced, but seemingly pleased with himself, the seasoned bull rider headed back to the rodeo, via the taco stand.

Lacy looked worried now. "Mac said I wasn't a smart little cowgirl to run off from Claire."

"No, you weren't." With obvious effort, Joel gave his daughter a stern look. "There are too many strangers here. You gave Claire a terrible scare."

"I know." Lacy's tears spilled over with her words. "I'm sorry, Joel. Mac said I'd be a good cowgirl if I said I was sorry."

"Just don't ever do that again." It was more of a plea than a scolding. Joel buried his face in Lacy's hair, rocking her gently, holding her tight. Megan blinked rapidly, relieved, yet feeling like the odd child left out of the circle, struck by how much it hurt to only stand and watch.

Then Joel turned and held out a hand to her. Her heart swelled until she thought it would burst. Megan hurried to his side, the grasp of his hand feeling warm and right.

"You okay?" Joel whispered.

"Yes. I am now." Megan wrapped an arm around Lacy, accepting the little girl's kiss in return.

"I wanted to take another picture of the ponies." Lacy touched her pink camera, looking contrite.

"You just have to remember to ask first." Megan smiled, wiping Lacy's tears away with her thumb, remembering the countless times her camera had led her astray as a kid.

Claire came rushing up with Jennifer then. "Thank heaven! Some wiry-looking, dark-haired cowboy told me you'd found Lacy. He said Lacy had described me to him."

"That was Mac," Joel explained, then he set Lacy down, advising her, "I think you have something to say to Claire, young lady."

"I'm sorry." Lacy had been frightened enough that there was no doubting her sincerity.

"You're forgiven, sweetheart. As long as the only thing lost were those ten years I didn't have to spare," Claire teased, glancing down the midway as she did. "Although that cowboy friend of yours seemed to think I was young enough to be Jennifer's mother. What did you say his name was, Joel?"

Claire gave her hair a pat. Megan laughed along with Joel, feeling a release of the tension that had gripped them. Once Claire had reluctantly left for home with Jennifer, Megan and Joel walked back down the midway with Lacy tucked safely between them.

But they couldn't completely shake the fright the little girl had given them. After a last, safe ride on the merry-go-round, they loaded Tally and started the trip back to Paradise.

Lacy was tired, and soon fell asleep, blond head cradled in Megan's lap, cowgirl boots resting on Joel's jeans. The ride home was quiet. But Joel's gaze seemed to seek Megan's as often as hers sought his.

So close a call.

So lucky.

The disbelief and relief seesawed between them and swirled in Megan's mind. When they neared her house, she just wasn't ready to let go. Her arm still curved protectively over Lacy, she urged Joel, "Let me follow you home in my pickup. I can get Lacy ready for bed while you take care of Tally."

"Lacy will be kind of crabby," Joel warned.

"I can handle that."

"Then I'd appreciate the help."

Lacy didn't wake when they stopped for Megan's pickup. After following Joel to his farm, Megan hurried over to open the passenger side of Joel's truck. Joel let the engine die and Lacy stirred, no longer lulled by the hum.

"Where's Ted?" Lacy squinted up at them, her small face thunderous.

Megan shot Joel a look that conceded he'd been right about the mood his daughter would be in. Then she pushed the pony from the edge of the seat until the fuzzy toy tickled Lacy's cheek. "Ted's right here."

Lacy tucked Ted under her chin and promptly rolled to her side and closed her eyes.

Megan laughed softly, brushing back Lacy's sunny bangs with her fingers. Tired and crabby, sweet and smiling, this child had come to be dear to her. Tracing the fullness of Lacy's cheek, she tucked errant strands of hair behind the small shell of the little girl's ear. She glanced up, about to ask if she should just carry Lacy in. Joel's tender expression had the words catching in her throat.

"Lacy cares about you, too, Megan."

She knew this had worried Joel before. Now she saw only gratitude in his eyes, and a flare of hope that started a reciprocating glow within her.

Lacy had awakened again at the sound of her name. She was struggling upright, her bottom lip thrust out. "I want a drink."

"You can have some water as soon as you get inside," Joel told her.

"I want soda."

"Uh—oh." Joel winked at Megan over top of Lacy's head. "Megan will be sorry she came to tuck you in if you're crabby."

Lacy shot Joel a petulant look. "I'm not crabby." She peered at Megan. "Are you really going to tuck me in?"

"I really am." Megan smiled as Lacy's small hand caught hers. "Come on. We'll let your dad tuck Tally in while we get you ready for bed."

Megan helped Lacy out of the truck. She started toward the house with Lacy leaning against her like a limp rag doll while Joel hurried ahead to unlock the door. When he'd left to go settle the horse for the night, Megan looked down at Lacy. The little girl's ponytail was tangled and dust was powdered across Lacy's clothes. It seemed a bath was in order.

Lacy was truly tired, inclined to fuss and complain. Megan indulged her with a little sympathy and teasing, shampooing the little girl's hair while Lacy sat in her tub of bubbles. In no time at all she had Lacy wrapped in a pint-size bathrobe. They went up to the pink-and-white bedroom to search for pajamas.

Megan smiled at the sight of wrapping paper and ribbon scattered over Lacy's rumpled bed. Joel and Lacy obviously had been in too big a hurry for bed-making that morning, but they'd found time to open birthday presents.

"Here's my new doll." Lacy picked up a doll half her size, a miniature of herself with blond ponytail and blue eyes. Lacy gazed admiringly at the doll's ruffled dress. "Joel's going to buy me a dress just like this. And he got me pink jeans for school."

Lacy pushed aside wrapping paper, looking for her new pants. Megan helped her, noting that both Lacy's gifts were from Joel. There'd been no mention of Luann, and she wondered about the gift he usually provided from Lacy's mother.

"I can't find my jeans." Frustrated, Lacy dropped the wrapping she held, giving a yawn that ended in a frown.

"Here they are." Aware Lacy was running low on energy, Megan praised Joel's choice of pink pants, then folded them neatly and placed them on the dresser next to the camera she'd given the little girl. "Let me find you some pajamas, sweetheart. By then, your daddy should be here to give you a good-night hug."

"He gives me a kiss, too." Lacy kissed her doll and tucked it beneath the covers.

Like a little mother. Megan thought of Luann and her smile turned bittersweet. She pulled open a dresser drawer, looking for pajamas with an unnecessary vigor.

"She looks just like me."

Megan turned from the dresser to find Lacy still standing beside the bed, staring at her doll.

"And I look like my mom."

Megan's heart took a painful beat and she suddenly wished for the power to stop the next few seconds, to change the course of Lacy's thoughts—thoughts she knew were headed in a heartbreaking direction. But there was no stopping time or changing the past and Megan stepped to the little girl's side, waiting, and praying for the right words to say. From downstairs, she heard the back door open and close. She hoped Joel would hurry. Lacy was going to need him now.

Lacy looked up then, her eyes brimming with unshed tears. "My mom forgot my birthday. She went away. She forgot me."

"Oh, Lacy, no." Megan knelt beside the little girl, wishing there were some way to absorb the child's all too familiar pain. Praying Joel had reminded Luann of Lacy's birthday, she soothed, "I'm sure she hasn't forgotten."

"Yes, she did," Lacy insisted fretfully.

Hot tears gathered in Megan's eyes. No wonder Joel had broken down and bought Lacy "presents'' from Luann. She reached for Lacy, wanting only to comfort.

But Lacy shoved her hands away. Grabbing the doll from the bed, she shouted, ''No! You're just going to go away, too!''

Shocked and hurt, Megan rose as Lacy ran off, pushing past Joel in the doorway. ''Lacy, wait!''

She started after Lacy, but Joel caught Megan's arm in a grip that stopped her cold. ''Let her go.''

Megan's gaze wavered between him and Lacy, finally settling on Joel after Lacy disappeared into his room. ''I have to talk to her—''

''What would you say? That you're staying?''

His words struck her as painfully as Lacy's had. A taut silence passed between them, then Joel released her, pushing a hand through his hair. When he spoke, his voice was laced with impatience, husky with need.

''I can't help wanting you to stay, Megan, any more than Lacy can. I tell myself I understand that you have to go. Then I touch you and you touch me and I don't understand at all. I can't help thinking we could work something out about your career, about your leaving for California.''

His words alternately thrilled her and made her want to cry. The decision to stay could be easily made; this man and his child had stolen her heart. But would it haunt her, never finding Patrice, never knowing if her mother regretted having left her and

Suzanne? Whatever the answer, Joel deserved to know that it would take more than her career to tear her away from him, or from Lacy. Haltingly, Megan tried to explain, "There's more to my leaving than starting a career."

"What do you mean?" Joel's low voice demanded.

"I think my mother is in California. When she left us, she had a plane ticket...." Megan looked away from his eyes, feeling responsible for the hurt she saw there, for the little girl crying down the hall.

"You want to find her."

"I always have...." But she could hear Lacy calling for Joel and she wasn't sure anymore.

"Lacy needs me. You'd better go." Joel sounded resigned.

"But Lacy—"

"I'll explain things to her." There was no censure in his voice. There was nothing. Nothing to indicate the pain in his eyes or the anger he must feel as he listened to Lacy crying.

Confused and uncertain, afraid anything she would say would only hurt him more, Megan left. She didn't know what else to do. All she knew as she was leaving was that she didn't want to go.

Upstairs, Joel heard the latch of the back door settle heavily into place. He went down the hall to his room. Lacy was curled on the bed with her doll, sobbing quietly now. He gathered her into his arms, his hand cupping Lacy's small bare foot as her arm stole around his neck.

Hearing the crunch of gravel below, he moved to the window. He wanted to call Megan back, to make her stay.

But she'd waited fifteen years to be able to leave.

Lacy laid her head on his shoulder and he rested his cheek on her hair.

He watched Megan go, knowing there was no chance of holding her now.

Chapter Ten

Megan raised her face from her arms folded across her knees, the night air drying the tears on her cheeks. From her perch on the porch step, she could see a sky awash in stars that outshone the sliver of moon. The crickets had quieted in the trees, leaving only the rush of the breeze through the branches, the sway and rustle of corn in the fields. She wondered how long she'd sat here; if hours or minutes had passed since she left Joel and Lacy. It seemed like years.

From a distance, the drone of a car reached her, the sound winding aimlessly through the night. She knew with a sudden certainty that she didn't want to be like that sound someday, not coming or going, but only drifting endlessly....

For fifteen years, she'd wondered and wished after Patrice, her whole future wrapped around going to California to search for her mother. But in the weeks since Joel's arrival, the feelings between them had grown until she felt that she had been waiting all these years for him to come home to her. Though she would never stop wondering about her mother, she knew she could live without Patrice. She didn't know how she would make it through this night without Joel, without Lacy.

Megan stared down the road over the sashaying stalks of corn, oblivious to the stars as she sought the familiar squares of light that shone from Joel's farm. But the lights at the Crawford house had ceased to glow and the darkness left her with a scared, empty feeling.

You make me feel like taking chances again, Joel had told her, and she'd seen the love in his eyes. Despite the pain of his past, he'd wanted, needed her. She was the one who could heal him, Megan thought fiercely.

But maybe he wouldn't trust her now, with his heart—or Lacy's.

Joel was leaving tomorrow afternoon for the rodeo in South Sioux City and Megan knew, after what had happened tonight, that he would be taking Lacy with him. Suddenly, she couldn't wait another moment to erase the hurt she'd seen in his eyes or the tears that had shone in Lacy's.

Megan rose from the step. As she ran to the truck, she pulled her keys from her pocket. Once inside, she struggled to fit the right key in the ignition. She was crying again, knowing she'd been a fool, praying Joel would understand, when headlights flashed in the rearview mirror, making her eyes blink and her heart miss a desperate beat. *Joel* . . .

But it wasn't. A large sedan came rolling up behind her pickup. The car was unfamiliar, but the figure climbing out and wrestling with his tie wasn't. Megan pushed open the truck door, realizing how much she needed to see her father. "Dad!"

"Meg!" Not missing the shine of tears on her cheeks, Matt folded his daughter into his arms, aware she held on too tightly. He hugged her back, thinking he'd come at the wrong time—and the right time.

Megan broke the embrace, swiping her face dry and leaning away to look at her father. "You look like that tie is choking you."

"I'll never get used to these." Matt tugged on the offending knot at his neck, thinking how much simpler life had been planting corn and putting bandages on his daughters' skinned knees. "I was hurrying to catch my flight and forgot to take the damned thing off."

"Here, I'll get it." Megan worked the knot free, sliding the tie from around her father's neck. "Why didn't you call and tell me you were coming? There's nothing wrong with Suzanne, is there?"

"No, no. Suzanne's . . . she's going to be fine." Matt cupped his daughter's tear-stained cheek. "You're the one I'm worried about, Meg."

"Oh, Dad." Megan caught her trembling lip, unable to claim his worry was unfounded.

He glanced at the pickup she'd just climbed out of. "That cowboy down the road have anything to do with those tears?"

"Yes. But through no fault but my own." Megan managed a small smile.

Matt nodded and retrieved his mangled tie from his daughter's fingers. "I'd probably be right if I guessed that meant your trip to California was part of the problem, too."

"Yes." In that moment, Megan wished she could tell her father everything, how she'd longed to find Patrice, how she'd been afraid of hurting Joel. How she'd hurt him, anyway. But she didn't want to hurt her father, as well.

With an arm around her shoulder, Matt herded her toward the house and they settled on the porch step. He reached over and ruffled her hair. "Remember all those nights we sat here eating ice-cream cones when you and Suzanne were kids?"

"I remember." Megan smiled wistfully, thinking how she'd shared that experience with Lacy in the same way she might have handed it down to a daughter.

Matt sighed, feeling the weight of his mistake more heavily than he ever had. "Megan, there's something I have to tell you. Something I should have told you long ago. Something you should know before you make any decisions."

"Dad, I've already—"

"Shh." As if she were a child again, Matt silenced her with a tap of his fingers to his lips. As if she were a child, Megan quieted. But there was nothing childlike about the unease creeping over her, seeing her father struggle for words, his face suddenly older, his gaze no longer meeting hers.

"The day your mother left—" Matt looked down at his folded hands, then started again, quietly confessing, "I never really knew my daughters until after that day. I can remember looking down at you and Suzanne—" Matt shook his head. "I was scared as hell."

Megan stared at her father. She remembered thinking how tall and imposing he had seemed. She and Suzanne hadn't really known him, either, but the last thing she'd ever suspected was that he'd been scared.

"I guess if any good ever came of Patrice's leaving me, it was what I found with you and Suzanne.

I fell in love with my little girls and I wanted to do my best to take care of you, not to let anything hurt you."

Her father's voice broke and Megan felt it in her heart. She placed a hand on his arm, her eyes burning. "We know that, Dad."

Matt patted her hand and pulled himself together. He didn't want her forgiveness based on pity. "I just want you to know that the wrong I've done wasn't intentional. I was only trying to protect you."

"What do you mean?" Again, unease rippled through her, intensifying as seconds ticked by.

"I know—I've always known—where your mother is."

A rush of emotion filled her, choked her, numbed her. *I've always known...*

Where? Why? Megan pressed her hands to her lips. She didn't know what to ask first. The longer she waited, with her own answers forming, the harder it became.

Matt ran his hands down his face. "She's in Los Angeles. She's remarried. Wealthy. Her husband owns a chain of high-class restaurants, which she decorated. They have no children. She—"

"Dad, stop." She couldn't stand the pain in his voice as he tried to tell her these things that didn't seem to matter at all. Only one question burned in her mind. Even as she asked it, she knew. "Why didn't you tell us?"

"It wasn't what she wanted, Meg." Matt watched his daughter bow her head, wishing she had stayed his little girl, wishing she'd never had to know, thinking maybe he'd only protected himself all these years, because it was killing him to see her this way. "Megan, don't cry."

But they both did. Then they sat beneath the stars, letting the breeze breathe new life into them.

Matt was braced for Megan's anger when she finally raised her head. "You should have told me. Told Suzanne. Maybe Patrice didn't want us back then, but over the years we might have changed her mind."

Matt didn't deny her the anger. But, as much as it pained him to tell her, he didn't lie to her anymore. "Every year since your mother left, I've sent her pictures of you girls. She knew when Suzanne got a concussion and when you both got your tonsils out. She has a copy of your report cards and your diplomas."

"She knows Suzanne was class valedictorian?"

"I sent her a copy of the speech."

And still no word from Patrice. Megan made herself ask, "Does she know about my pictorial in the children's magazine?"

"I sent her the issue."

Megan fought it, but her face crumpled, the tears falling again. She felt her father's arm come around her, and she leaned into him, letting him rock her, the hurt she'd felt all these years pouring out. "I wanted to accomplish so much, to impress her. To find her and have her love me."

"I know, Meg. I know."

Her father's voice was filled with understanding and Megan leaned away, looking up at him in question.

"Your best pictures have always been of ordinary people and places, not the glitter and glamour you insisted you had to find in California."

He knew her well. Megan realized this had been hard on her father, too. The years of living with his lie were etched in his face. "Does Suzanne know?"

"I've told her." Matt sighed heavily. "She's in counseling. We agreed it was best she didn't start college under the pressure of all that perfection."

Megan let the words soak in. "That was her way of coping?"

"I'm afraid so."

"How could I miss that? I should have seen—"

"Megan, don't do that to yourself. I'm the one who should have seen, not you."

But Megan couldn't help feeling guilty. She remembered the day Suzanne had told her to leave the doll Lacy had played with lying on the bed, how out of character that had seemed. *Don't try to be someone you're not,* Suzanne had said. Yet her sister had quietly done so all these years. "Suzanne was so much like Patrice. I envied her, wanted to be like her."

Matt ran a hand over Megan's hair, so like her mother's. "I can't look at you and not see Patrice. And your knack with the camera, you got that from your mother. Patrice was very artistic." He didn't add that his ex-wife had felt her talent was stifled by the simple country life he had to offer back then.

"Thanks, Dad." She could handle this, Megan thought. But what about Suzanne? "Is the counseling helping Suzanne?"

"It seems to be. She knows we love her, and that's what matters most." Matt straightened. "By the way, she wanted me to give you a message. Something about one of those dolls of hers. She wants Lacy to have it."

Megan felt a measure of relief with his words. "Dad, she's really going to be okay."

"I think so, too." Matt shifted, pulling a paper from his shirt pocket. He hesitated, then held it out to her. "This is your mother's phone number and address."

Megan looked down at the paper. Once again, she thought he should have told her and Suzanne years ago about their mother. But her father's hand was trembling and she knew he'd suffered just as much as she had. She thought of Lacy, about her feelings for the child, and realized how much. Megan reached out and curled her father's fingers over the paper. "Why don't you hang on to that for a while?"

Matt frowned. "I understand if you still want to go to California. I'll do what I can to make it easier."

"Thanks, Dad. Maybe someday." Megan gazed down the road toward the Crawford farm. "But first, I think I'd like to go to South Sioux City."

The lane to Joel's farm was just ahead. Megan checked her braided hair in the rearview mirror and smoothed her white shirt. She centered the western belt buckle, decorated with a roping horse and rider, at her waist. A small overnight bag lay on the seat beside her. The cooler weather had held for another day, but Megan's palms were sweaty when she signaled her turn.

She drove up near the house and got out of the truck. Over by the barn, Joel was in the process of hitching the trailer to his pickup, Lacy sitting on his lap behind the steering wheel as he backed up the truck. They climbed out together and went to secure the hitch before turning to acknowledge her presence.

Lacy wrapped an arm around Joel's leg and they stared across the yard at her, reminding her of the way they had looked in her shop that first day Joel had come back to Paradise. She now knew the full strength of the bond they shared. Knew she wanted to share it, too.

But they made no move toward her, and she felt her courage fading beneath their blue-gray gazes until she had to turn away. Megan opened the truck door and reached in to unzip her overnight bag, taking out the picture of Joel that Lacy had snapped with her camera. Drawing a deep breath, she faced them once more.

This time, Lacy let loose of Joel's leg and came running over. The breath shuddered out of her lungs and Megan's heart lifted. Lacy skidded to a stop before her.

"Are you coming to the rodeo with us?" Lacy eyed Megan's belt buckle with approval.

"I want to."

"Even though I was bad?"

"Oh, Lacy." Megan knelt and hugged her. "You weren't bad. I think you were just scared that I would leave and not come back."

"Do you still need to go to that place?"

"No. I don't need to." Everything she needed was right here in Paradise. "Why don't you take this picture and sign your name on it for your dad? Can you do that?"

"I can do it. I'll sign it like he signed my birthday card. I'll use my crayons." Lacy took the picture and, with a last big smile, ran to the house.

When Megan looked over, Joel was standing near the trailer, his weight rocked to one booted foot. Beneath his hat brim, his hair shone like gold against the black collar of his shirt, his hands tucked into snug jean pockets. He lifted his face, the sun glancing off his perfect features, his blue eyes rivaling the sky. *A cowgirl's dream...*

She was ready to make promises now.

Megan crossed the yard and stopped before him, her mouth dry and her heart hammering beneath his steady gaze. "I gave Lacy the picture of you that she took."

"Thanks. Lacy will like that. That camera you gave her is her favorite birthday present."

Joel looked toward the house into which Lacy had disappeared. Megan waited, sensing there was something more he wanted to say about his daughter. After a moment, he told her, "I've called Lacy's mother. I told Luann it was up to her to come through for Lacy's birthday. That if she wants to see Lacy, I'll arrange it. Lacy's still waiting to hear from her."

Megan's heart ached at the pain in his voice. But she thought of her father and the lie they had all lived with and said softly, "You've done the right thing."

"I'm trying." Joel caught her gaze and held it. "I understand now that Lacy won't find any peace until she comes to terms with her mother's desertion."

What was he trying to tell her? Megan stared up at Joel, all at once filled with dread and hope. He thought she would be leaving Paradise. Was he letting go, or saying he would be here waiting when she came back?

Joel reached out then, and touched the small square of silver at her waist, sending a hot wave of longing through her. His gaze met hers in question, and the wariness she saw there gave her the courage to respond.

"I was thinking—" her voice wavered at the same time her heart missed a beat "—that I'd like to do a pictorial essay on the life of a rodeo cowboy—"

Her words were lost, muffled against Joel's shirtfront as his arms came around her, pulling her close, his face buried in her hair.

"I wouldn't care if you took pictures on the moon as long as you came home to me." He drew back, catching her face in his hands. "Megan, you made me see how Lacy was hurting over Luann. I can understand that you want to go to find Patrice. If you need me, I'll go with you."

Megan touched his face. "You'd do that for me?"

"I love you. I'd do anything." Joel kissed her, the touch of his lips sweet with promise, his hands sliding upward to rest alongside her breasts, sending shivers through her.

Megan wound her arms around his neck and whispered, "I was coming back last night, you know."

Joel chuckled. "I was going to stop at the tack shop on my way out of town and kidnap you."

"I love you, Joel. I knew if there was anyone in this world I couldn't live without, it was you. And Lacy."

"It won't be easy with Lacy," Joel said, sighing and leaning back to look down at her.

"I can help her."

"We'll help each other."

She knew he referred to Patrice. It was time now, to tell him that her mother had never wanted her. Megan looked down at Joel's arms, clasped warmly around her. She would always feel the pain of her mother's desertion, but this time, there was no shame, only regret. "Last night, when I was leaving to come back here, my dad came home. He told me the truth about my mother. That he's known all along where she was. She just never wanted me or Suzanne."

"Ah, Megan." Joel's arms tightened around her and Megan allowed herself the luxury of a few more tears before she put the past behind her.

"I'm okay." Megan felt Joel's kiss on her hair, then surprisingly, heard him laugh. She raised her head from his chest and his gaze directed hers downward. Megan stifled a giggle at the sight of Lacy's small face, staring indignantly up at them.

"I want a hug, too."

Joel hauled the little girl up between them and they kissed and tickled her until she begged to be let down.

"You made me drop my picture," Lacy scolded, catching it before the breeze could send it cartwheeling across the yard. She handed it to Joel, then demanded of Megan, "Are you coming with us?"

"You bet I am."

"I have to go tell Tally." Lacy ran off, and Megan grinned at Joel. But his gaze was riveted to Lacy's photo and she moved to his side, curious to see what had put that wondrous look on his face.

Joel stared down at the photo, not at his image, but at the carefully made letters Lacy had printed across the bottom.

To Daddy. Love Lacy.

Joel traced the letters, his hand trembling. He hadn't known it would mean this much to him. He had the assurance of Lacy's love. And the promise of Megan's.

Joel grasped Megan's hand. He hadn't planned on falling in love again, for his sake and Lacy's. But last night, after Megan had gone, he'd realized he was ready to take chances again. Now it seemed love had been here all along, just waiting for him to come back to Paradise and claim it.

He wouldn't be alone anymore. And there would be someone to share the joy and pain of raising his daughter.

Together, Joel and Megan turned to watch Lacy skip through the tall grass along the pasture fence.

Their hearts lurched in unison when she fell.

*   *   *   *   *

WILD RIVER

by
Laurie Paige

Maddening men...winsome women...and the untamed land they live in—
all add up to love! Meet them in these books from Silhouette Special Edition
and Silhouette Romance:

WILD IS THE WIND (Silhouette Special Edition #887, May)
Rafe Barrett retreated to his mountain resort to escape his dangerous feelings
for Genny McBride...but when she returned, ready to pick up where they
left off, would Rafe throw caution to the wind?

A ROGUE'S HEART (Silhouette Romance #1013, June)
Returning to his boyhood home brought Gabe Deveraux face-to-face
with ghosts of the past—and directly into the arms of sweet and loving
Whitney Campbell....

A RIVER TO CROSS (Silhouette Special Edition #910, September)
Sheriff Shane Macklin knew there was more to "town outsider"
Tina Henderson than met the eye. He saw a generous and selfless woman
whose true colors held the promise of love....

Don't miss these latest Wild River tales from Silhouette Special Edition
and Silhouette Romance!

SEWR-4

Take 4 bestselling love stories FREE

Plus get a FREE surprise gift!

Special Limited-time Offer

Mail to Silhouette Reader Service™

3010 Walden Avenue
P.O. Box 1867
Buffalo, N.Y. 14269-1867

YES! Please send me 4 free Silhouette Romance™ novels and my free surprise gift. Then send me 6 brand-new novels every month, which I will receive months before they appear in bookstores. Bill me at the low price of $2.19 each plus 25¢ delivery and applicable sales tax, if any.* That's the complete price and—compared to the cover prices of $2.75 each—quite a bargain! I understand that accepting the books and gift places me under no obligation ever to buy any books. I can always return a shipment and cancel at any time. Even if I never buy another book from Silhouette, the 4 free books and the surprise gift are mine to keep forever.

215 BPA ANRP

Name	(PLEASE PRINT)	
Address	Apt. No.	
City	State	Zip

This offer is limited to one order per household and not valid to present Silhouette Romance™ subscribers. *Terms and prices are subject to change without notice. Sales tax applicable in N.Y.

USROM-94R

IT'S OUR 1000TH SILHOUETTE ROMANCE, AND WE'RE CELEBRATING!

JOIN US FOR A SPECIAL COLLECTION OF LOVE STORIES BY AUTHORS YOU'VE LOVED FOR YEARS, AND NEW FAVORITES YOU'VE JUST DISCOVERED. JOIN THE CELEBRATION...

April
REGAN'S PRIDE by **Diana Palmer**
MARRY ME AGAIN by **Suzanne Carey**

May
THE BEST IS YET TO BE by **Tracy Sinclair**
CAUTION: BABY AHEAD by **Marie Ferrarella**

June
THE BACHELOR PRINCE by **Debbie Macomber**
A ROGUE'S HEART by **Laurie Paige**

July
IMPROMPTU BRIDE by **Annette Broadrick**
THE FORGOTTEN HUSBAND by **Elizabeth August**

SILHOUETTE ROMANCE...VIBRANT, FUN AND EMOTIONALLY RICH! TAKE ANOTHER LOOK AT US! AND AS PART OF THE CELEBRATION, READERS CAN RECEIVE A FREE GIFT!

YOU'LL FALL IN LOVE ALL OVER AGAIN WITH SILHOUETTE ROMANCE!

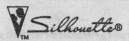

CEL1000

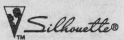

It's our 1000th
Silhouette Romance™,
and we're celebrating!

And to say "THANK YOU" to our wonderful readers, we would like to send you a

FREE AUSTRIAN CRYSTAL BRACELET

This special bracelet truly captures the spirit of CELEBRATION 1000! and is a stunning complement to any outfit! And it can be yours FREE just for enjoying SILHOUETTE ROMANCE™.

FREE GIFT OFFER

To receive your free gift, complete the certificate according to directions. Be certain to enclose the required number of proofs-of-purchase. Requests must be received no later than August 31, 1994. Please allow 6 to 8 weeks for receipt of order. Offer good while quantities of gifts last. Offer good in U.S. and Canada only.

And that's not all! Readers can also enter our...

CELEBRATION 1000! SWEEPSTAKES

In honor of our 1000th SILHOUETTE ROMANCE™, we'd like to award $1000 to a lucky reader!

As an added value every time you send in a completed offer certificate with the correct amount of proofs-of-purchase, your name will automatically be entered in our CELEBRATION 1000! Sweepstakes. The sweepstakes features a grand prize of $1000. PLUS, 1000 runner-up prizes of a FREE SILHOUETTE ROMANCE™, autographed by one of CELEBRATION 1000!'s special featured authors will be awarded. These volumes are sure to be cherished for years to come, a true commemorative keepsake.

DON'T MISS YOUR OPPORTUNITY TO WIN! ENTER NOW!

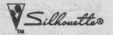

CELOFFER

CELEBRATION 1000! FREE GIFT OFFER

ORDER INFORMATION:

To receive your free AUSTRIAN CRYSTAL BRACELET, send three original proof-of-purchase coupons from any SILHOUETTE ROMANCE™ title published in April through July 1994 with the Free Gift Certificate completed, plus $1.75 for postage and handling (check or money order—please do not send cash) payable to Silhouette Books CELEBRATION 1000! Offer. Hurry! Quantities are limited.

FREE GIFT CERTIFICATE   096 KBM

Name:_____

Address:_____

City:_____State/Prov.:_____Zip/Postal:_____

Mail this certificate, three proofs-of-purchase and check or money order to CELEBRATION 1000! Offer, Silhouette Books, 3010 Walden Avenue, P.O. Box 9057, Buffalo, NY 14269-9057 or P.O. Box 622, Fort Erie, Ontario L2A 5X3. Please allow 4-6 weeks for delivery. Offer expires August 31, 1994.

PLUS

Every time you submit a completed certificate with the correct number of proofs-of-purchase, you are automatically entered in our CELEBRATION 1000! SWEEPSTAKES to win the GRAND PRIZE of $1000 CASH! PLUS, 1000 runner-up prizes of a FREE Silhouette Romance™, autographed by one of CELEBRATION 1000!'s special featured authors, will be awarded. No purchase or obligation necessary to enter. See below for alternate means of entry and how to obtain complete sweepstakes rules.

CELEBRATION 1000! SWEEPSTAKES
NO PURCHASE OR OBLIGATION NECESSARY TO ENTER

You may enter the sweepstakes without taking advantage of the CELEBRATION 1000! FREE GIFT OFFER by hand-printing on a 3" x 5" card (mechanical reproductions are not acceptable) your name and address and mailing it to: CELEBRATION 1000! Sweepstakes, P.O. Box 9057, Buffalo, NY 14269-9057 or P.O. Box 622, Fort Erie, Ontario L2A 5X3. Limit: one entry per envelope. Entries must be sent via First Class mail and be received no later than August 31, 1994. No liability is assumed for lost, late or misdirected mail.

Sweepstakes is open to residents of the U.S. (except Puerto Rico) and Canada, 18 years of age or older. All federal, state, provincial, municipal and local laws apply. Offer void wherever prohibited by law. Odds of winning dependent on the number of entries received. For complete rules, send a self-addressed, stamped envelope to: CELEBRATION 1000! Rules, P.O. Box 4200, Blair, NE 68009.

 ONE PROOF OF PURCHASE

096KBM

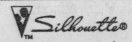